The Road Home

Don't Miss

MARGUERITE HENRY'S

Ponies *of* Chincoteague

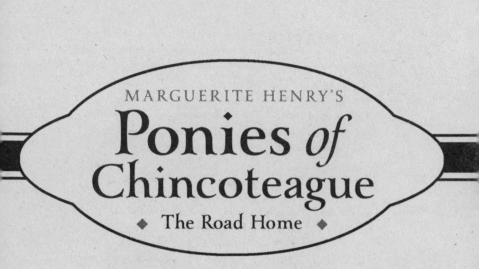

MARGUERITE HENRY'S

Ponies *of* Chincoteague

◆ The Road Home ◆

CATHERINE HAPKA

Aladdin

New York   London   Toronto   Sydney   New Delhi

ALADDIN

An imprint of Simon & Schuster Children's Publishing Division
1230 Avenue of the Americas, New York, NY 10020
First Aladdin paperback edition April 2017
Text copyright © 2017 by The Estate of Marguerite Henry
Cover illustration copyright © 2017 by Robert Papp
Also available in an Aladdin hardcover edition.
All rights reserved, including the right of reproduction in whole or in part in any form.
ALADDIN and related logo are registered trademarks of Simon & Schuster, Inc.
For information about special discounts for bulk purchases, please contact
Simon & Schuster Special Sales at 1-866-506-1949 or business@simonandschuster.com.
The Simon & Schuster Speakers Bureau can bring authors to your live event.
For more information or to book an event contact the Simon & Schuster Speakers Bureau
at 1-866-248-3049 or visit our website at www.simonspeakers.com.
Book designed by Karina Granda
The text of this book was set in Adobe Caslon Pro.
Manufactured in the United States of America 0317 OFF
2 4 6 8 10 9 7 5 3 1
Library of Congress Control Number 2016953806
ISBN 978-1-4814-5997-6 (hc)
ISBN 978-1-4814-5996-9 (pbk)
ISBN 978-1-4814-5998-3 (eBook)

The Road Home

◆ CHAPTER ◆
1

"EASY, BREEZY," NINA PERALT EXCLAIMED as her pony charged toward the fence they were supposed to jump—a small vertical.

Bay Breeze flicked an ear back toward her. Nina steadied him with her legs and reins, and then leaned forward as he sprang over the vertical with several inches to spare.

When she landed, Nina heard a laugh from the other end of the riding ring. "You're a poet and you don't even know it," her friend Jordan called out. She was sitting on her lease horse, a cute Appaloosa gelding named Freckles, waiting for her turn to jump.

"Easy, Breezy," their riding instructor, Miss Adaline,

echoed with a chuckle, shaking her head so her pink-tinted dreadlocks bounced. "That's not something I hear you say often, Nina. He's lively today, eh?"

Nina brought Breezy back to a walk, then headed toward the others. "Definitely." She patted Breezy's neck. "I like it!"

She'd owned the stout little Chincoteague pony for almost two years, ever since her parents had surprised her with him for Christmas. She adored everything about him, from his brown and white spots to his cheerful disposition. She had to admit that he was a little on the lazy side most of the time, though.

But it was spring, and Miss Adaline said that sometimes made horses feel perkier than usual. That certainly seemed to be true in Breezy's case.

The instructor was pointing at the third rider in the lesson, a red-haired girl on a dark bay lesson horse named Ringo. "You're up, Leah," Miss Adaline said. "Go ahead and jump the same line the other two just did."

"Go, Leah!" Nina cheered as she took her place beside Jordan and Freckles.

Nina and Jordan had been riding in the same Tuesday afternoon lesson for more than a year. Leah had joined the group during the winter after a couple of other girls had dropped out or switched times. But Nina had known her even before that, since the two of them attended the same small private school just outside the French Quarter.

"Settle down, buddy," Nina murmured. Leah had just sent her lesson horse into a canter and now Breezy was shifting his weight as if eager to follow.

Jordan looked over. "He really is lively today," she said. Then she giggled as Nina's pony dropped his head and let out a loud sigh. "Well, for Breezy, anyway."

Nina laughed, then tucked a stray strand of curly black hair back under her helmet, and shaded her eyes against the bright afternoon sun to get a better view as Leah and her mount jumped the line of fences. It was only the beginning of May, but it was already hot and sunny in New Orleans.

"Good job, Leah," Miss Adaline said as Leah rode over to the others after finishing the exercise. "Okay, now let's put those lines together into a little course. . . ."

The rest of the lesson went well, and Nina was in a good mood as she slid down from the saddle and pulled the reins over Breezy's head. As she led the pony toward the barn, Jordan and Leah were right behind her with their horses.

"That was fun," Jordan said, giving Freckles a pat.

"Yeah. But listen, let's find a place to untack together." Nina grinned at her friends. "I have some big news I'm dying to tell you guys!"

Leah's green eyes instantly went sharp and interested. "Gossip?"

"Not exactly." Nina's grin got even wider. "Just come on and you'll find out soon enough."

Before long all three of their mounts were cross-tied in the stable aisle. As soon as she finished clipping Breezy's halter to the ties, Nina stepped over to undo his girth.

"Well?" Leah demanded. "What's your big news already?'

Jordan giggled. "Yeah, you wouldn't want us to die of suspense, right?"

Nina considered torturing them by keeping them waiting a little longer. Jordan was famously excitable, while Leah loved gossip and secrets and was usually one of the first people at school to know all the latest news. It would be fun to mess with both of them.

But not this time. Nina was practically bursting with her news and needed to share it immediately.

"Okay," she said, pulling Breezy's saddle off his back and setting it on the floor beside her grooming tote. "You know I just had my birthday, right?"

"Just?" Leah cocked her head. "Um, I was at your party, you know. It was at least three weeks ago."

"Me too," Jordan chimed in. "But whatever. Is this about your super-secret surprise gift?"

Nina giggled and grabbed a brush out of her tote. "I should've known you'd remember that." She started running the brush over Breezy's body, which made him flap his lip with pleasure. "Yeah, my parents finally told me what it is."

At her party, her parents had given her several nice gifts—a cute saddle pad for Breezy, a new leotard for her dance class, and a cool antique bracelet she'd been eyeing in a local shop. But they'd also promised her one more big gift—one she'd have to wait to find out about. And that morning at breakfast, they'd finally spilled the beans.

"So what is it?" Jordan asked. "A new saddle?"

"Or a pair of real diamond earrings like that girl at school just got?" Leah guessed.

"Ooh! Or maybe a whole new designer wardrobe," Jordan put in.

"Nah." Leah shook her head. "Nina wouldn't even want something like that, or diamond earrings, either. It's probably something like a gift certificate to one of those crazy old junk shops on Magazine Street she likes so much."

By then, Nina was laughing so hard she almost dropped the brush she was using. "If you two would shut up, I might be able to tell you!" she exclaimed. "Then again, if you'd rather just spend all day guessing . . ."

"No, no." Jordan grabbed her arm, smiling at her pleadingly. "Tell us—please?"

"Okay." Nina swiped at a sweaty spot on Breezy's coat. "You'd never be able to guess, anyway. See, my parents said they're taking me and three friends of my choosing to the Big Easy Equine Expo!"

Leah wrinkled her nose. "The what?"

But Jordan gasped. "Oh, I heard about that!" she cried. "They're having it at Fair Grounds Race Course in a couple of weeks." She spun to face Leah. "It's, like, this huge event sort of like a state fair or something, except instead of cows and vegetables or whatever, it's all about horses! There's supposed to be tons of horsey shopping, plus riders doing demonstrations of all kinds of cool stuff and, like, parades of different breeds, and who knows what else."

"Wow!" Leah's eyes widened. "That sounds pretty cool."

"I know, right?" Nina grinned at both her friends. "And guess what? Two of those three tickets have your names on them!"

"Really?" Jordan shrieked, startling the horses. Ringo merely lifted his head, while Breezy barely bothered to flick an ear toward the noise. But Jordan's own horse, Freckles, took a few steps sideways, yanking on the cross-ties.

"Ho, Freckie." Nina stepped to the Appaloosa gelding's head and gently pulled him forward a step or two until the pressure on the halter abated. "Jordan, you'd better not let Miss Adaline catch you spooking the horses, or she'll make you ride the whole next lesson without stirrups!"

Jordan waved her hand to brush away Nina's comment. "Never mind that," she said. "I'm so psyched that you're bringing us, Neens!"

"Me too." Leah looked excited. "The Expo will be the perfect place to shop for those new paddock boots my parents promised me!" She held up one foot and waggled it. "Check it out—these are practically falling apart."

Leah's boots looked perfectly fine to Nina—barely broken in, really. But she didn't bother to say so. She and Leah were total opposites in some ways, including their clothing preferences. Nina liked to browse the local secondhand shops for unique vintage looks, while Leah preferred buying brand-new outfits in the latest styles. But that was okay with Nina. She liked having all different types of friends. It made life more interesting.

"You guys will have to help me figure out who to give the third ticket to," she said. "I haven't decided yet."

Jordan giggled. "Maybe you should give it to one of your imaginary friends."

Nina stuck out her tongue at her friend as Leah laughed. Jordan was referring to the Pony Post, a private website Nina had set up with three other girls to talk about their beloved Chincoteague ponies. The other three members all lived far away—Maddie Martinez was from northern California, Haley Duncan lived on a farm in rural Wisconsin, and Brooke Rhodes was in southern Maryland, just a short drive from Chincoteague Island itself—so Nina had never met them in person. But she checked in with them online almost every day, and occasionally spoke to one or all of them on the phone. They were as much her friends as the two girls standing in front of her, though nobody else seemed to understand that. Nina didn't really mind, though. What she had with the Pony Post was extraordinary, and she didn't much care what other people thought of it.

"Watch it! I could give all three tickets to my imaginary friends, you know." Nina grinned as the other girls laughed. But at the same time, she found herself briefly imagining what that would be like. Haley was sure to love anything at the Expo that had to do with eventing, the sport she did with her Chincoteague pony, a spunky bay pinto named Wings. But she was pretty much game for anything, often entering local Western competitions, which meant she'd be sure to love learning more about other horse activities too, from parade riding to saddleseat. Meanwhile Brooke would probably spend the whole time trying to memorize every fact and tip they heard to add to her endless knowledge of horses and ponies. That knowledge came in handy, not only when her friends had a question, but also when it came time to take care of her young chestnut mare, Foxy, who lived in her backyard. As for Maddie? It was hard to guess. Maybe she'd want to shop for a matching saddle pad and polo wraps for the Chincoteague lesson pony she rode, Cloudy, who was the spitting image of the title character in Marguerite Henry's classic book, *Misty of Chincoteague*. Or maybe Maddie would want to skip shopping to try to see every possible demonstration and clinic she could. Whatever she did, she'd definitely have fun—and she'd make sure her friends did too.

Nina smiled at the thought of how much the Pony

Posters would love the Expo. But she shook it off as Jordan and Leah thanked her again for the invitation. Sure, it would be stupendous to spend a day like that with her Pony Post pals. But she was sure to have a great time with her local friends too.

"I know who you could invite with that third ticket." Leah shot Jordan a smirk, then turned it on Nina. "Jordan's cute older brother."

Jordan spun around. "Ew, no way!" she exclaimed. "You can't ruin my day at the Expo by inviting that jerk Brett. Did I tell you he ate all the cereal in the entire house and didn't tell anyone?"

"No boys allowed," Nina said quickly, bending to dig through her grooming tote to hide the pink blush spreading over her cheeks. Why did thinking about Brett make her feel so funny? And how did Leah even know about that, anyway? Nina certainly didn't spend any time talking about boys the way some of her friends did. . . .

"Whatever." Leah shrugged, nudging Nina with her shoulder. "You could ask Trinity."

"I thought about her." Nina was relieved by the change

of topic. "She's an obvious choice since she's one of my best friends. But she's not into horses at all."

"Yeah." Jordan nodded. "Trin's cool and all. But you should definitely bring someone who's going to appreciate the Expo."

They spent the next few minutes discussing options while they groomed their ponies, carefully brushing away dried sweat and saddle marks. After a while, Leah started to look bored.

"Listen, not to change the subject . . . ," she began.

"But you're going to?" Nina finished with a grin.

Leah rolled her eyes. "You'll thank me when you hear the latest gossip," she said. "I almost forgot to tell you, I heard a new girl is starting at our school tomorrow. Our grade, even."

"Seriously?" That really was big news. There were only about forty kids in their whole class. "Boy or girl?"

"Hope it's a boy," Jordan put in, though she didn't sound particularly interested, probably because she attended the local public school and only knew a few of Nina and Leah's classmates.

"It's a girl," Leah replied. "I heard her family just moved back to New Orleans from somewhere overseas. Oh, and her name is Edith. Isn't that weird? Sounds like an old lady, not a kid our age."

Nina shrugged. "I like it—it's different."

"You like anything different," Jordan teased. "But listen, let's continue this chat out on the levee, okay? I want to take Freckie out there for a snack."

Nina nodded immediately. Breezy, Freckles, and Ringo were city ponies who lived in their stalls much of the time, only getting turned out for short periods to stretch their legs in small dirt paddocks. Cypress Trail Stables fed them plenty of hay, but the only time the horses got to eat grass was when their riders took them out to graze on the grassy expanse of park facing the Mississippi River. Nina tried to get Breezy out there as often as possible.

"Okay, let's go," she agreed, dropping her hoof pick into her tote.

"I'm in, too," Leah said, already reaching for Ringo's lead rope.

The three of them were leading the ponies toward

the door when a buzz came from Leah's pocket.

"Your pants are ringing," Nina joked.

Leah fished her cell phone out of her pocket with her free hand. "It's my mom," she said when she glanced at the display. "Better see what she wants."

"Nice phone," Jordan whispered, leaning closer to Nina while Leah spoke to her mother. "Think it's new?"

"It is," Nina confirmed. "She mentioned it at lunch the other day."

Just then Leah hung up and turned to face them, looking annoyed. "I'll have to take a rain check on the levee," she said. "My parents want me home right away." She rolled her eyes. "Mom was all dramatic about it too."

"Is everything okay?" Nina asked.

"Probably." Leah tucked her phone back in her pocket. "Sometimes my parents like to remind me that I'm the kid and they're the adults, you know? I'm sure they're just mad because I forgot to load the dishwasher or something."

"Guess Ringo will have to settle for hay today." Jordan reached over to give the bay gelding a pat. "See you Saturday at our next lesson, Leah."

"Yeah." Leah gave a tug on Ringo's lead. "And I'll see you at school tomorrow, Neens. Don't forget to check out the new girl!"

"See you." Nina waved as Leah hurried off toward Ringo's stall.

She and Jordan continued down the aisle with their ponies. As they stepped out into the humid afternoon, Jordan glanced back over her shoulder. "How much do you think that phone of hers costs, anyway?" she said.

Nina blinked at her. "What's with you and Leah's phone?" she said with a laugh. "It's just a phone, okay?"

"Not exactly." Jordan rolled her eyes. "I saw the same phone in a magazine. It costs like three times what my parents paid for mine!"

Nina shrugged, not really liking Jordan's disapproving tone. "So what? Leah's parents can afford it," she said, reaching over to adjust Breezy's halter as they turned to follow a trail leading under a shady canopy of live oaks draped with Spanish moss. "Her mom is a scientist, and her dad and his business partner have great jobs working with all the big banks."

"Exactly." Jordan shot her a look over Freckles's withers. "She's loaded. And I'm sure you must've noticed how she makes sure everyone knows it. Do you really want to waste one of those Expo tickets on her? Maybe you should ask her to pay for her own ticket. Then you could invite two people whose parents don't own half of New Orleans."

Nina frowned, tempted to tell Jordan she was sounding like a bigger snob than Leah could ever be. Instead, though, she took a deep breath and forced a playful smile.

"Don't be a hater," she said lightly. "Otherwise I might be tempted to do what I said earlier and use all three tickets on my imaginary friends."

That made Jordan giggle. "Okay, sorry," she said. "I take it all back, okay? You have to let me come! It's going to be a blast, right?"

"Totally." This time Nina didn't have to force her smile. "I can't wait!"

♦ CHAPTER ♦
2

WHEN NINA OPENED THE FRONT DOOR OF her house, she automatically stuck one foot out to stop her family's two Siamese cats from dashing outside. But for once, they weren't lurking there waiting for her.

She soon guessed why when she heard voices and laughter drifting out from the kitchen. It sounded as if some of her relatives had stopped by.

Nina's father's side of the family could trace their history back through New Orleans for more than two hundred years. Gabe Peralt was the youngest of five children, which meant that Nina had lots of cousins, though they were all much older than she was. Most of the family gathered every

Friday night for a big family dinner, but that didn't stop various aunts, uncles, siblings, and cousins from dropping in on one another whenever the mood struck.

After kicking off her boots near the door, Nina hurried across the front room and peeked into the small but airy kitchen. "Hi, everyone," she said.

Her cousin Kim looked up from chopping carrots at the counter. She was one of Nina's favorite relatives, and not only because she was a dance instructor who had taught Nina for years. Kim was almost exactly the same age as Nina's father, even though he was technically her uncle, and the two of them had grown up together having adventures all over the Seventh Ward and beyond. Nina loved hearing the stories from their childhood, which seemed to grow wilder and more humorous with every retelling.

Beside Kim was her mother, Nina's aunt Vi, who was helping Nina's mother with something on the stove. The cats, Bastet and Teniers, were twining themselves around the humans' legs and letting out an occasional piteous yowl.

"Nina!" Aunt Vi exclaimed, gently shoving Teniers away with one foot. "You're just in time to set the table."

Nina's mother nodded, swiping a wispy strand of light brown hair off her forehead. "Your father just texted to say he's on his way home from work," she said. "We'll eat as soon as he gets here."

"I'll come help in a sec, okay?" Nina said. "I want to change out of my riding clothes first."

"Good idea," Kim said with a laugh. "We've been working hard on this food, and we'd rather not have the kitchen smell like a barn."

Nina laughed too, and then continued down the long, narrow hall that bisected their hundred-year-old cottage. Her room lay between the kitchen and her mother's art studio, which was at the back of the house.

It took only a moment to shed her jods, socks, and sweaty riding T and pull on a cool, full-skirted sundress she'd found in one of her favorite vintage shops. Then she grabbed her laptop, which she'd left on the bed right after school. She knew her family wouldn't mind if she took an extra few minutes to check in with the Pony Post—especially since she had such big news for them.

When she logged in, Nina saw that all three of her friends had posted after school. She scanned their entries.

[BROOKE] Hi, guys! Just waiting for Kiersten to get here—she's coming over to help me teach Foxy some dressage stuff she learned in her lessons before she moved here. Can you believe it? Me and Foxy, getting all fancy, ha! I'll let you know how it goes after.

"I can believe it," Nina murmured aloud, feeling proud of her friend for trying something new. Brooke had done almost all of Foxy's training herself so far, which was a lot, since the chestnut mare had been a yearling when Brooke had bought her at the annual pony auction in Chincoteague, Virginia. Brooke might not enter as many competitions as Haley or take as many lessons as Nina or Maddie, but that didn't mean she didn't work hard on her riding.

Nina glanced at the next entry, which had posted an hour and a half after Brooke's.

[MADDIE] Sounds cool, B! U and Foxy can do anything, and don't u forget it!!! As for me, I only wish I could ride today. I forgot to take out the trash and my rotten sis tattled on me, so I'm grounded. Grrr! O well, I'll be back at the barn soon. . . .

[HALEY] Hi, everyone! Brooke, you'll love dressage! I thought it was boring at first, but it's actually pretty cool! Anyway, I'm just posting to show u all the pix of Wings that my cousin took yesterday. Isn't he cute?

Nina smiled as she scrolled down to the photos. In most of them, Haley and Wings were jumping various obstacles, from a pile of logs to a gate stuffed with brush. With help from her family, Haley had built a pretty substantial cross-country course to practice on in one of their cow fields.

When she reached the end of the photos, Nina opened a new text box and began to type.

[NINA] Hi, all! Brooke, psyched to hear more about

yr dressage lesson. H, Wingsie looks adorable

as always! I just had a lesson—B was a superstar.

He had tons of energy today (for a change, lol).

Anyway, I don't have much time, so I'll tell u more

about my lesson later. Rt now I have to tell u the big

news I've been dying to share all day. . . .

Her fingers flew over the keyboard as she filled them
in on her parents' Expo surprise. She also told them that
she'd already invited Jordan and Leah, and still needed to
figure out who to bring with the third ticket.

[NINA] I wish I could just bring one of you, lol! Actually

I wish I could bring all 3 of you! Wouldn't that be

stupendous?? Anyway, gtg—I'm supposed to be

helping with dinner. Will check in l8r so u can all tell

me how jealous you are of my fab b'day gift, ha ha ha!

Still smiling at that, she signed off and then headed
back toward the kitchen.

◆ ◆ ◆

"Is that your phone buzzing, Nina?" Kim said.

Dinner had ended a few minutes earlier, and Nina was rinsing plates in the kitchen while her cousin wiped down the counters. She stepped over and glanced at her cell phone, which she'd left on a wooden chair nearby.

"Yeah, it's a text from my friend Jordan," she said after scanning the readout.

Kim nodded. "Right, the cute little girl you ride with who's afraid of everything?"

Nina laughed. "She's not afraid of *everything*," she corrected as she opened the text. Then she smiled. "Good news! Her parents said she can come to the Expo."

"Cool," Kim said. Over dinner, Nina and her parents had told Kim and Vi all about Nina's surprise gift. "What about the other girl you invited?"

"Leah? Hmm, I don't think she's texted me about it yet. That's kind of weird." Nina scrolled through her recent texts to make sure she hadn't missed any. "Usually she's on her phone all the time—especially since she got her new one. Maybe her parents are working late or something."

She frowned, realizing that didn't make sense. Leah's mom had called her home while they were still at the barn, so Leah should have had a chance to ask about the Expo right away. Then again, maybe Leah was right and her parents were annoyed with her about something, which would explain why she might not have asked them yet. . . .

Deciding not to worry about it, Nina stuck her phone in her pocket and got back to work. When she and Kim had finished up in the kitchen, Kim wandered off to join the other adults on the front porch, while Nina headed to her room, eager to see if the rest of the Pony Post had read about her news.

Her laptop was still on the bed where she'd left it. Nina flopped down beside it and flipped it open. When she logged in, she saw that all three of the other Pony Posters had checked in since her last visit.

[MADDIE] Great photos, Haley! U and Wingsie always look so professional when ur jumping. Not like me and Cloudy, lol. Usually I look like I'm about to fall off over even a teensy x-rail!

[BROOKE] Ya, cute shots, H. I can't believe some of the stuff you jump, you're way braver than me, ha ha! Nina, sounds like a good lesson today, and fun news from ur parents.

[HALEY] Thx, guys! Wings looks good in pics, right? So do all our ponies actually! Which reminds me, Nina, didn't u promise us just yesterday that u would take pics at yr next lesson? We haven't seen Breezy in ages!

Nina realized that Haley was right. She'd been so distracted by the news about the Expo that she'd forgotten all about that promise.

Speaking of the Expo . . . Nina scanned back through her friends' latest posts, wondering if she'd missed something. But no—other than Brooke's brief mention, none of them had said anything about her big news.

"That's weird," she murmured, scrolling farther up to make sure her own message had posted. There it was, just as she remembered, right above her friends' latest postings. So why hadn't they said anything about the Expo? She had been so sure they'd be just as excited as she was herself. . . .

"Nina? I'm heading out." Kim poked her head in Nina's half-open bedroom door. "See you tomorrow, right?"

"Yeah." Nina took a lesson at Kim's dance studio every Wednesday night. "I'll be there."

Her cousin took a step into the room. "Hey, you okay? You look troubled."

Nina glanced up with a smile, amazed that she'd noticed. Then again, Kim could pinpoint a dancer's tiniest loss of balance or slightest flaw in position. Why would Nina doubt that she could spot a perplexed mood just as easily?

"I was just looking at the Pony Post." Nina's entire family knew all about the website and enjoyed hearing updates at most Friday-night dinners. "I told them all about the Expo earlier, and I was expecting a ton of questions and excitement and stuff. But it's like they barely paid attention to what I said."

"Hmm." Kim came closer, bending over to peer at the

laptop screen. "What'd you say, sweetie? Maybe you made it sound so good that they're a touch envious."

Nina snorted. "Envious? No way, they're not like that."

Kim shrugged. "Just saying, not everybody is as lucky as you are, Nina. Don't ever forget that, okay?"

"Sure." Nina waved good-bye as her cousin headed out.

Then she sat there for a moment staring into space. Could Kim be right? Had Nina bragged too much about her fantastic birthday gift?

"No," she whispered. Then she shook her head. "Maybe?"

After all, Kim was right—not everybody was as lucky as Nina, with a great pony and generous parents who were able to surprise her with fabulous stuff whenever they felt like it.

Scrolling back up, Nina studied each of her friends' names in turn. Maddie's parents made a comfortable living, but having four kids in the family meant that Maddie didn't always get everything she wanted.

Then there was Brooke, who had paid for Foxy with

her own money and still paid a large share of the pony's expenses. And Haley, who had to scrimp and save to afford lessons and competitions.

"Oops," Nina said aloud, reaching out to pat Bastet as the cat leaped gracefully onto her bed, followed by Teniers. "Maybe I did brag a little," Nina told the cats, pulling her laptop away just before Teniers strolled across the keyboard.

Nina propped the computer on her pillow and stared at the screen. Should she apologize to her friends for bragging?

Then she shook her head, deciding that might only make things worse. "This is one of those times when it's kind of hard having imaginary friends," she told Teniers, scratching his favorite spot under his chin. "It would be a lot easier to smooth things over if I could just talk to them face to face like I can with my local friends. . . ." She sighed, then blinked. Speaking of her local friends, she still hadn't heard from Leah about the Expo.

Nina shut her computer down and pulled her phone out of her pocket. She sent Leah a quick text asking if she'd talked to her parents yet, then sat there petting the cats and waiting for a response.

Ten minutes later none had come. Nina finally shook her head and set the phone aside.

"Guess she's busy tonight or something," she said, rolling onto her back so Bastet could walk onto her stomach as she loved to do. "That's okay, I'll just talk to her at school tomorr—eep! That tickles!"

Dissolving into laughter, she grabbed both cats in a big group hug.

◆ CHAPTER ◆
3

"HEY, PERALT!" SOMEONE CALLED AS NINA emerged from the musty back stairwell into the second-floor hallway of her school.

She waved over her shoulder without bothering to see who it was. She'd just spotted a familiar cloud of wavy red hair ahead.

"Yo, Trin!" she yelled. "Hold up, girl!"

Her friend Trinity turned and waved. "What's up, Nina?" she said. "Did you hear there's a new girl?"

"Yeah." Nina had all but forgotten about Leah's gossip, but she wasn't really focused on what Trinity was saying. "Listen, have you seen Leah?"

"Not yet. Why?" Trinity fell into step beside Nina as they headed toward their lockers, which were both located in one of the school's crooked back hallways. Their school was a converted Greek Revival mansion and it retained much of the charm of the original building, from the columns on the porch to the third floor dormer windows.

"I need to talk to her about something. No biggie." Nina didn't say anything about the Expo. Trinity wasn't the type of girl to be offended if she wasn't invited—especially since she had virtually no interest in horses—but Nina didn't want to say anything until she'd decided what to do with that last ticket. "Guess I'll catch up with her in homeroom."

But when she stepped into the classroom, Leah's seat was empty. A bunch of kids were gathered around a desk near the back of the room, but Nina didn't spot Leah's sleek auburn hair in the crowd there, either.

"Check it out." Trinity was looking the same direction. "That must be her?"

"Where?" Nina blurted out, before realizing that Trinity wasn't talking about Leah. "Oh, the new girl. Right. Let's go say hi."

She pushed her way through the crowd. A girl was perched on the edge of a desk, looking as comfortable as if she'd been attending the school since kindergarten the way Nina and most of the other kids gathered around her had. She was petite, with big brown eyes, a heart-shaped face, and a sleek dark bob.

"Nina!" A boy named Jacob looked up with a smile. "Did you meet Edith yet?"

The girl laughed. "I told you guys, call me Edie," she exclaimed. "Edith's my grandmama." Her voice had an extra little lilt on top of her regular local accent that made her sound exotic.

"Hi, Edie," Nina said. "I'm Nina Peralt. Welcome to New Orleans."

"Welcome back, you mean," another girl interjected. "Edie grew up here."

Edie nodded, making her shiny brown hair bounce. "I was born here, and I've lived here off and on my whole life," she explained. "My parents are both diplomats, which means we move around a lot—mostly overseas. But still, New Orleans is home, you know?"

"I hear you." Nina couldn't help liking the new girl. She had a friendly, open way about her that made Nina pretty sure she'd fit right in. "So welcome back, then."

"Thanks." Edie pointed. "Hey, cool bracelet."

Nina lifted her arm, making the bracelet she was wearing jangle. It was a silvery chain with a several dangling horse head charms. "Thanks. I found it in this neat little shop over in Metairie."

"Cool. Are you into horses, or did you just like the bracelet?"

"Oh, Nina's definitely into horses." Trinity rolled her eyes, while several of the other kids laughed. "Don't get her started!"

Edie laughed too. "Hey, that's awesome," she said. "I love horses! I try to do some riding in every country we visit. My favorite was riding an Andalusian in Spain. It was amazing!"

Several of the other kids looked impressed. Nina felt the same way, though she also couldn't help flashing back to what Kim had said the evening before. Would Jordan— or other people, like the Pony Posters—think that what

Edie had just told them was snobby, or merely interesting and exotic? Was it really bragging if it was true?

Nina tuned back in when she realized everyone was staring at her, becoming vaguely aware that Edie might have just spoken to her. "Um, sorry?" she said.

"I said, do you have a horse of your own?" Edie asked.

Nina nodded, all thoughts of snobbery flying out of her mind. "Yeah, I have a pony named Bay Breeze—Breezy for short," she said, warming up quickly to her favorite subject. "He's a Chincoteague pony—that means he came from this little island up in Virginia, where they round up the wild ponies once a year and—"

"Yeah, I know!" Edie broke in, sounding excited. "I must've read *Misty of Chincoteague* a zillion times when I was younger. That's so cool! I've never even met a real Chincoteague pony before."

"You'll have to come out to the barn sometime." Nina smiled warmly, tempted to mention the Pony Post, since Edie seemed so interested in the breed. But she didn't feel like listening to Trinity and the others tease her about her imaginary friends, so she decided to save that for another time. "But anyway, riding in Spain, huh? That's incredible," she said instead. "What other countries have you lived in?"

"Oh, we never actually lived in Spain," Edie said with a shrug. "We just went down there for a vacation while Mom was posted in Paris, and . . ."

From there, Edie regaled them with tales of her life in France, Scotland, Morocco, and various other places until the teacher came in and called the class to order.

"See you guys next week!" Nina waved as the last few members of the dance class headed for the door with their bags slung over their shoulders.

When they were gone, Nina walked over and slipped her bare feet into a pair of flip-flops lying beside her own gym bag. Then she glanced over at Kim, who was by the window jotting some notes on a pad.

"I'll start sweeping up," Nina called.

Kim glanced up, blowing a strand of hair out of her face. "Thanks, sweetie. I'll help in a sec."

Nina's class was the last one of the evening, so she

usually stuck around to help Kim tidy up in exchange for a ride home. As a bonus, that usually meant that Kim ended up staying for dinner.

Humming under her breath, Nina hurried to the closet and grabbed a couple of brooms. She left one of them leaning against the barre, then started sweeping with the other one. After a moment Kim tossed her pad aside and picked up the second broom.

"Good class tonight," Nina told her cousin with a smile. "I'm going to be sore tomorrow!"

Kim laughed. "That's always my goal," she teased with a wink. "So what's new since last night?"

"Lots, actually." Nina was sweeping near the big plate glass window that formed the far wall of the studio. Noticing a smudge on the glass, she rubbed at it with the hem of her T-shirt. "There's a new girl at school. Her name's Edie, and she just moved back here from Paris."

"Interesting."

"Yeah, she is," Nina said. "But I didn't even tell you the best part yet. She's into horses!"

Kim chuckled. "What are the odds? You seem to find

them everywhere—here in New Orleans, off in California, all over the Internet . . ."

"What can I say? I have a gift," Nina joked. Then she frowned slightly. "Oh, and speaking of horses—there's some other news, too, if you can call it that. I still haven't found out if Leah is coming to the Expo or not."

"What do you mean?" Kim shot her a confused look. "Didn't you ask her about it at school today?"

"She was absent." Nina leaned on her broom. "Nobody knew why."

Kim raised her eyebrows. "Ooh, a mystery!" she said jokingly.

"It really is," Nina insisted. "I mean, she didn't seem sick at all when I saw her yesterday at the barn. And she didn't say anything then about being out." She blinked. "Although she did get a weird call from her parents while we were grooming."

"Weird how?"

Nina shrugged, trying to remember exactly what Leah had said about the call. "Her parents insisted she come home right away. She wasn't sure why. Do you think that might have something to do with her being absent today?"

Kim laughed again. "I think you've been watching too many spy movies with your dad, that's what I think," she said. "Gabe always did love a good conspiracy."

Nina laughed weakly, but she couldn't help feeling vaguely troubled. "It just seems strange, that's all. Even if she suddenly came down with a cold or something, why wouldn't Leah at least text me back?"

"If she's not feeling well, she's probably not thinking about that right now," Kim said.

"You're right, I guess." Nina started sweeping again. "Thanks. I just really want to make sure she can come. Then all I have to do is figure out who to invite for the third ticket."

"I'm sure you'll come up with someone," Kim said. "I've never seen a girl with so many friends. Real and imaginary." She winked again.

Nina stuck out her tongue at her cousin. "Speaking of my imaginary friends, thanks for that, too."

"For what?"

"You know—what you said last night." Nina sighed.

"After you left I realized I probably was bragging a little too much when I told them about the Expo. At least I'm guessing that's got to be why they didn't say much about it."

"Hmm." Kim glanced at her, looking thoughtful. "Online communication can be tricky."

"Tell me about it." Nina shook her head. "I always say that the Pony Posters are just as much real friends as everyone here in New Orleans. And that's true." She swept a stray scrap of paper toward the little pile of debris the two of them were forming in the center of the room. "But our friendship can be a little different sometimes, since we communicate mostly through the written word."

Kim nodded, stepping over to the closet and pulling out a dustpan. "I hear you."

"Anyway, it's hard sometimes." Nina started sweeping the debris pile toward the dustpan Kim was holding. "But don't get me wrong—they're totally worth it, of course. I wouldn't trade my Pony Post friends for the world." She laughed. "Sometimes I just wish I could move them all here to New Orleans!"

Kim chuckled. "That would be fun."

"Yeah." Nina pictured it for a second, smiling at the thought of trail riding through Audubon Park with Haley, Brooke, and Maddie. It would be a parade of Chincoteague ponies! "It would be awesome to have them here where I could see them every day in person." She shrugged. "Then again, if they lived here, I wouldn't get to hear all their cool stories about the places they live and the different stuff they do with their ponies."

"True," Kim agreed. "Like Gramma Rose always says, every dark cloud has a silver lining. Now come on, let's finish up and get out of here, girl. A little bird told me your dad might be making corn bread tonight."

The intoxicating scent of fresh corn bread filled the house when Nina and Kim entered a short while later. Nina's father glanced up from the oven when they looked in. Even though he worked full time as a successful attorney and part time as an amateur musician in a jazz band, he still found time to indulge in his love for cooking at least a few times per week.

"You're just in time!" he said. "Should be ready to eat in ten."

"Excellent." Kim smacked her lips. "I'll set the table." She headed over toward the plate cabinet, pausing to pat the cats, who were camped out on the bench by the refrigerator.

"Be back to help after I change clothes," Nina promised.

Her father nodded, swiping the sweat off his brow with a dishrag. "Grab your mother on your way back," he said. "She's in the studio."

It only took Nina a minute to change out of her leotard. She pulled on shorts and a tank top, and then headed down the hall to her mother's art studio.

Nina's mother was bent over a lump of clay, but she looked up when Nina came in. "Is the food ready?" she asked. "I can smell it all the way back here."

Nina sniffed the air, realizing she was right. Normally the studio smelled of wet clay, cleaning supplies, and a touch of her mother's favorite gardenia-scented cologne. But today the smell of corn bread was overpowering even here at the very back of the house.

"Dad said it's almost ready," Nina said.

"Good. I'll put this clay away and be right there."

Nina nodded and headed back out into the hall. She started toward the kitchen, but paused by the open door to her room. Her laptop was on her bed, and despite her grumbling stomach, she couldn't resist going in and flipping it open. Kim wouldn't mind setting the table by herself, and Nina hadn't checked in with the Pony Post all day. . . .

Soon she was logged in and scanning the latest entries.

[BROOKE] Hi, all! Can't ride today, it's raining here, boo! So you should all tell me stories about yr ponies so I feel better!!

[HALEY] Hi, Brooke! Just heading out for a cross-country lesson at my trainer's place. I'll be sure to write u all about it later! Hope u can hold out until then, lol!

[MADDIE] Sounds cool, Hales! We all might have to live thru yr riding today, ha! I have soccer and won't have time to go to the barn. And I think today is Nina's

dance class, right, N? So she probably won't ride

today either. Oh well, there's always tomorrow, right?

Nina chewed her lower lip. It was hard not to notice that none of her friends had mentioned the Expo at all. Had she really been that annoying when she'd told them about it?

Just then she heard her father calling her name. "Coming!" Nina hollered back. Then she typed quickly:

[NINA] Only have a sec! But ya, dance tonight, no

riding. Can't wait to hear about your ride tho, Haley,

be sure to fill us in asap! Ttyl, gtg!

She scanned the words she'd just typed, feeling a little strange. Normally she would have told them about Leah's odd disappearing act and her worries about finding the best person to present with that third Expo ticket. But if they didn't want to talk about it, she wasn't going to force the issue. At least not yet.

I just hope they get over it by the time the Expo gets here, she thought as she logged off and headed for the kitchen. *Because going to the Expo won't even be as much fun if I can't share it with three of my best friends afterward!*

• CHAPTER •
4

"YOU'RE HERE!" NINA BLURTED OUT WHEN she turned the corner toward her locker on Friday morning and saw Leah standing there talking to Trinity. "Wow, Leah, I was starting to think you'd transferred schools or something."

Leah shot her a sour look. "Sorry I didn't alert the media," she muttered. "I was sick, okay?"

"Okay." Nina blinked at her. Leah could be prickly sometimes, but she seemed extra cranky today. Then again, she'd never dealt that well with pain or illness. Back in fourth grade she'd sprained her ankle playing kickball, and had complained nonstop about it for at least three months.

"Glad you're back, dude," Trinity told Leah. "Want to look at the math homework?"

"That's okay, I'll get it later." Leah slammed her locker shut and slung her purse over her shoulder. "I have to hit the bathroom. See you."

Nina opened her mouth to say something, but Leah was already disappearing around the corner. She shrugged and glanced at Trinity. "So what was wrong with her, anyway?"

"She didn't really say." Trinity spun the combination on her own locker. "She didn't have much to say at all, actually."

"Maybe she's still not feeling well." Nina bit her lip, glancing in the direction her friend had disappeared. "I need to talk to her about something, though. See you in homeroom, okay?"

She hurried to the nearest girls' bathroom. Leah was inside, staring at herself in the cracked, cloudy old mirror over the twin pedestal sinks.

"Hi," Nina said. "You ran off so fast I didn't get to ask you—did you talk to your parents about the Expo?"

Leah met her gaze in the mirror for a second, then looked away. Her expression was frosty. "Actually, I've had other things on my mind. Like being sick. So lay off, okay?"

Nina took a step back, startled by the testiness in Leah's voice. "Sorry," she said. "I didn't realize you were that sick."

Leah turned and pushed past her, not meeting her gaze. "Why else would I be out for two whole days? Duh, Nina, use your brain for a change."

With that, she slammed through the door and stormed off, leaving Nina standing there with her mouth hanging open.

"So you never got to talk to her about the Expo?" Jordan shot a look down the stable aisle. She and Nina were tacking up their ponies for their Saturday-morning lesson.

"I tried." Nina adjusted Breezy's girth. "She just kept blowing me off. And she didn't answer my text last night, either."

"And now she's late for our lesson." Jordan checked her

watch. "We'd better get moving, or Miss Adaline will be mad."

Ten minutes later, Nina and Jordan were mounted and walking their ponies around the ring to warm up. Miss Adaline was leaning against the fence, periodically glancing toward the entrance to the barn to look for Leah.

"Where is that girl?" she exclaimed at last. "We're going to have to start without her if she doesn't get her behind on a horse soon. I have lessons to teach after this and I don't want to be running late the whole day long because Leah decided to sleep in."

Nina winced. "She's probably just a little behind. She was sick this week," she told the instructor, allowing Breezy to drift to a halt.

Miss Adaline pulled her cell phone out of her pocket. "Well, let's see if she's planning to grace us with her presence today."

As Miss Adaline made her call, Nina traded a worried look with Jordan, who had stopped Freckles nearby. Where was Leah? She might have her quirks, but before now she'd always been on time for lessons.

"Maybe she's sick again," Jordan murmured. "What did she have, anyway?"

"I don't know." Nina shook her head. "She didn't say."

"Huh?" Jordan looked perplexed. "What do you mean, she didn't say? Didn't you talk to her at all?"

"I tried." Nina shrugged. "She wasn't exactly in a superchatty mood."

A moment later, Miss Adaline hung up with a frown. "No answer," she told Nina and Jordan. "That's it, then. Let's start without her. If she shows up, we'll figure out what to do with her." She smiled and rubbed her hands together. "Two or three laps at rising trot without stirrups might remind her to be more prompt. . . ."

Nina laughed, then urged Breezy into a walk. When Miss Adaline called for a trot, Nina squeezed both legs against the pony's sides. A few strides ahead, Freckles surged into a trot. But Breezy just kept walking.

"Trot, boy," Nina said, squeezing again, then adding a little kick with her heels. "Trrrrot!"

Finally the pony lumbered into a slow trot. Miss Adaline was watching.

"He looks a bit sluggish today," she called. "You'll have to be stronger with your aids."

Nina nodded, already out of breath from squeezing with every stride to keep her pony from slowing down again. "So much for all that energy from the other day. I guess his spring fever passed already."

She couldn't help being a little disappointed by that. This was her first chance to ride since that fabulous lesson on Tuesday afternoon, and she'd been hoping that Breezy would be equally lively. But it seemed he was back to his usual lazy self—even worse than usual, if anything.

"Just keep after him," Miss Adaline said. "He might perk up as we go along."

But Breezy remained lethargic throughout the ride, barely managing to heave himself over the jumps and dropping from a canter or trot to a walk or halt anytime Nina stopped pushing him for more than a second.

By the time she dismounted and ran up her stirrups, Nina was feeling a little worried. "Do you think he's okay?" she asked Miss Adaline, who was helping Jordan loosen

Freckles's girth nearby. "It's kind of hot today. Maybe he's coming down with something."

"I doubt it." The riding instructor cast a critical eye over the pony, who was standing quietly with his head hanging low. "But he does look kind of blah, doesn't he? Let's check his vitals—just in case."

Nina led the pony inside and untacked him while Miss Adaline fetched a thermometer and a stethoscope from the tack room. But when the instructor checked his temperature and heart rate, she declared him well within normal bounds.

"Guess he was just feeling pokey today," she said, giving Breezy a pat. "Or maybe he overdid it so much on Tuesday that he's still a little tired or sore. We'll check him again tomorrow, but I wouldn't worry about it." She smiled at Nina. "You just have a lazy pony, that's all."

Nina was relieved. She fed the pony a chunk of carrot, which he gobbled eagerly. Then she grabbed a brush and went to work on the mark her saddle had left on Breezy's spotted coat.

Jordan was combing Freckles's mane in the next set of

cross-ties. She glanced over at Nina as Miss Adaline hurried off.

"I guess Breezy isn't sick," she said. "I was afraid he'd caught whatever mystery illness Leah had."

Nina chuckled, then shook her head. "I can't believe Leah just ditched our lesson." She dropped her brush in her grooming tote, then fished her phone out of her pocket. "Maybe I'd better check on her, see what's up."

She sent Leah a text, then waited a moment, staring at her phone in case there was an immediate reply. But none came, so she stuck the phone back in her pocket.

"Nothing?" Jordan peered at her over Freckles's back.

"Nope, not yet." Nina sighed. "I wonder what's wrong."

"Maybe she lost her brand-new fancy phone and her parents grounded her," Jordan said with a laugh. "That would explain why she's not texting you back. And why she's so cranky, too."

Nina smiled weakly. Jordan didn't seem too worried, but she hadn't known their lesson-mate as long as Nina had. It just wasn't like Leah to pull a no-show for something she loved as much as she loved riding.

"I hope she's not sick again," Nina murmured. Her eyes widened as a new thought occurred to her. "Especially not *really* sick, if you know what I mean."

"What, like with a disease or something?" Jordan wrinkled her nose thoughtfully. "Do you think she might be?"

Uh-oh. Jordan was a worrier by nature. Nina didn't want her to overreact and start telling everyone that Leah had malaria or polio or the black plague or something. "Probably not," she assured Jordan quickly. She bent down and fished a hoof pick out of her tote. "Anyway, we definitely shouldn't borrow trouble, like my gramma always says. I'm sure Leah will be in touch when she feels like it."

"Sorry you can't come to the show tonight, Boo." Nina's father gave a tug on her ponytail. "No minors allowed in this club."

"It's okay." Nina tried to attend as many of her father's band's performances as she could. But sometimes, like tonight, they had gigs at bars or clubs where all patrons had to be at least twenty-one years old. Besides that, it was Sunday, so Nina had to get up early for school the next day.

"Dinner's in the fridge." Her father went to the mirror over the console table to straighten his tie. "There's leftover gumbo, or you can make yourself a sandwich with that chicken from Friday."

Nina nodded, glad that her parents trusted her to stay home alone when they went out, even on weekends when the family's long-time maid, Delphine, was off. Some of her friends weren't so lucky, and a few even still had babysitters come over when their parents went out.

She glanced toward the hallway at the sound of high heels click-clacking on the tile floor. Her mother had just emerged, looking beautiful in a slinky emerald-green dress and glittery sandals. Both cats were trailing along behind her, probably hoping to rub some of their fur off on her outfit.

Nina let out a wolf whistle. "Wow, you guys are going to be the best-looking couple there," she exclaimed.

Her father smiled and stepped over to put an arm around his wife. "You really think so?"

"The best-looking couple over sixty, anyway," Nina amended, straight-faced.

Her mother laughed, then waggled a finger at Nina. "Just for that, you're grounded, young lady," she joked. "Seriously, don't stay up too late, okay? It's a school night."

"I know, I know." Nina picked up her father's trumpet case and handed it to him. "And I'm not allowed to eat candy and soda for dinner, either."

Soon her parents were on their way. Nina fed the cats, but she'd stopped at her favorite coffee house for a snack on the way home from the barn, so she wasn't hungry yet. She headed to her room, where she grabbed her laptop and then continued out to the tiny walled garden behind the house.

She settled herself in one of the cast-iron patio chairs and logged on to the Pony Post. None of the others had posted since the last time she'd checked in, so she opened a new text box and started to type.

[NINA] Hi, all! Went to the barn this afternoon like I told you I might. B looked fine so I saddled up for a quick trail ride. But as soon as we got going, I could

tell he was feeling lazy again. I asked him to trot, and
he barely managed three strides before he dropped
back to a walk again. It was like riding molasses!

She posted that much, then scrolled back to read it over, feeling worried anew as she thought back over the day's ride. Breezy was always lazy, but these past two rides had been way beyond that. Nobody at the barn seemed to think there was anything wrong with him, but Nina knew her Pony Post friends would understand her concern.

[NINA] I was kinda worried, so I gave up on riding and
got someone to help me check his temp and stuff
again. He still seemed fine—just tired I guess. So I
decided to give him a nice, long grooming session to
make him feel better. By the time I finished he looked
so shiny and clean and perfect he was ready to be
in a show or something, ha! Then I walked him out to
the closest place with grass and let him eat a while.
That perked him up, lol!

She hit enter, and her words appeared on the screen below the others. Nina chewed on her lip, staring at a bird fluttering around in the vines on the garden wall and wondering if she really was making too big a deal out of her pony's recent behavior. Maybe if he hadn't been so perky on Tuesday, she wouldn't even have noticed when he went back to being pokey.

Then she blinked as another text box appeared on the screen below hers.

[BROOKE] Nina, u still on??

With a smile, Nina quickly opened another blank box. The Pony Posters all had such different schedules in their different time zones that they only occasionally ended up on the site at the same time. But it was always nice when it happened—a happy accident, as Nina's grandmother liked to say.

[NINA] I'm here! How r u? Did u ride Foxy today?

She waited, and Brooke's response came within a couple of minutes.

> [BROOKE] Ya, just a trail ride—ground is too wet
> from all the rain to do much jumping or ring stuff.
> But never mind that. U sound worried about BB—
> do u think he's OK?

That made Nina smile again. She'd long since decided that Brooke was the most thoughtful and sensitive of the four of them, often noticing when someone was in a funny mood or thinking of ideas that never would have occurred to the others.

> [NINA] I don't know what to think. He seems to
> be as healthy as a—well, u know! But he's just so
> LAZY! I mean he's always lazy, but. . . .

> [BROOKE] U know him best. If you think
> something's wrong u should trust ur instinct.
> (But don't panic, lol!)

[NINA] Lol! U know as much about horse health and stuff as anyone I know. Do u have any ideas? What could turn a slightly lazy pony into a total slug?

[BROOKE] Hmm, dunno. If he was sick he'd prolly have a temp or something, you know? Maybe it's just cuz he's getting older.

[NINA] Maybe. But he's only 11 yrs old! Lots of ponies and horses I know are older than that and not slowing down at all. Like Haley's Wings, for instance. And nobody would ever call HIM lazy, lol. . . .

[BROOKE] OK then do u know if they've changed anything about his feed lately? Or got a new kind of hay? Sometimes that can make a diff. . . .

They continued to speculate together for several more posts, but nothing Brooke suggested seemed like a likely cause of Breezy's lazy attitude. Finally Nina decided it was time for a change of topic.

[NINA] I'm sure he's probably fine and I just got

spoiled by that nice lesson earlier this week,

ha ha! But even if he's not sick, I'm a lil worried that

someone else I know might be...

She went on to share Leah's absence from school and her moody behavior the day before. The more she typed, the more worried she felt. Breezy might be acting a little out of character lately, but Leah's behavior was even more bizarre.

[BROOKE] Wow, that's crazy. I hope she's OK. But

I'm sure she'll talk to u eventually, right?

[NINA] Sure, I guess. The trouble is, I need to know

if she's coming to the Expo. It's only 2 wks away

now and I want to have time to figure out someone

else to bring if she's going to blow it off!!

[BROOKE] Oops, sorry, my stepdad's calling me to

feed Foxy, gtg. Hang in there, OK?

[NINA] OK, thx for listening!

She waited, but there was no further response from Brooke, and Nina guessed she'd already signed off. She did the same, then wandered out to the kitchen to fix herself some dinner.

✦ CHAPTER ✦
5

ON MONDAY BEFORE HOMEROOM, NINA
was trying to find her English book in the mess at the
bottom of her locker when she felt a tap on her shoulder. She spun around, hoping it was Leah. Nina had never
received a reply to her texts over the weekend, so she still
didn't know why Leah had missed their lesson. She also
still didn't know whether Leah was coming to the Expo,
and she wanted to find out before she invited anyone else.

But it wasn't Leah standing there. "Oh!" Nina blurted
out. "Edie. Hey, what's up?"

The new girl smiled at her. "Happy Monday. How was
your weekend? Did you ride?"

"Yeah," Nina said. "Well, sort of."

Edie cocked her head, looking amused. "Sort of? You *sort of* rode? What does that mean?"

Nina laughed. "Sorry, that sounded weird, didn't it? See, my pony was superlazy in our lesson on Saturday, so on Sunday I didn't really ride for long."

"Is he always so lazy?" Edie leaned against the next locker. "That's the worst. I rode this huge draft cross in Ireland once who was so lazy I thought my legs were going to fall off. Anytime someone tells me riding isn't a real sport because the horse does all the work, I think of that guy!"

Nina laughed again. "Breezy's always lazy, just not quite this lazy," she said. "But it's okay—my legs are strong from years of dance class."

"You dance?" Edie sounded interested. "What style?"

"All of them, pretty much." Nina finally spotted her English book. She grabbed it and then slammed the locker door shut. "My cousin is a dance instructor, and I've taken every style she teaches—jazz, contemporary, hip hop . . ."

They spent the next few minutes chatting about dancing and ponies and various other topics. Nina had never had much trouble talking to anyone about anything, but Edie was especially easy to talk to. Nina was about to suggest they head for homeroom when she glanced up and saw Leah approaching.

"Leah!" Nina called, waving. "Hi, I've been trying to reach you." She shot Edie an apologetic look. "Can I catch up to you in homeroom? I really need to talk to Leah about something."

"Sure, no worries." With a little wave, Edie hurried off down the hall. She smiled and said hi to Leah when she passed her, but Leah didn't seem to notice. Nina couldn't help thinking that Leah looked kind of haggard.

"You feeling okay?" Nina asked, stepping closer. "You look kind of, I don't know, tired."

"Gee, thanks." Sarcasm dripped from Leah's voice. "Just what every girl loves to hear on a Monday morning."

Nina cleared her throat. "Um, sorry. I just meant—"

"Whatever," Leah interrupted. "Now, excuse me. I have to hit my locker before I'm late."

"Okay, but we need to talk." Nina broke into a jog to keep up as Leah rushed toward her locker. "Are you sure you're okay? When you didn't show up for lessons the other day, we were kind of worried. Plus you still haven't given me an answer about the Expo—"

"Sorry," Leah snapped, not sounding sorry at all. "I happen to have more important things on my mind right now than some stupid Expo, okay?"

Nina wasn't sure how to respond to that. "Um, okay," she said. "It's just that it's less than two weeks away now, and . . ."

She let her voice trail off, since Leah had just put on a burst of speed, leaving her behind. Nina stopped where she was, deciding not to try to catch up.

Leah doesn't seem to be in the mood to talk, she told herself, turning and wandering slowly back toward her homeroom. *Does that mean she doesn't want to go to the Expo? Is that why she's acting weird?*

But that didn't make sense. Leah wasn't exactly shy—if she didn't want to go, she wouldn't hesitate to just come right out and say so. Besides, she loved everything about horses and riding. Why in the world wouldn't she want to go to the Expo?

Nina stopped short again, hugging her books to her chest as another thought struck her. Had she been right the other day when she'd worried that her friend might be sicker than she was letting on? What if Leah really did have some terrible disease and wasn't telling anyone?

"Yikes," Nina whispered to herself.

Then the bell rang, startling her out of those unsettling thoughts. After one last glance back in the direction Leah had gone, Nina took off at top speed so she wouldn't be late for homeroom.

Once again, Leah managed to avoid Nina and their other friends for most of the day, disappearing into the library during lunch and arriving at most of her classes just as the bell rang. The more Nina observed her friend's behavior, the more uneasy she felt.

She was still thinking about Leah when she arrived at the barn after school. Their next group lesson was the following afternoon. Would Leah show up this time? If so, maybe Nina could talk to her then.

When she turned into the aisle where Breezy's stall

was located, she saw her riding instructor coming toward her with a bridle slung over her shoulder and a saddle balanced against her hip.

"Hi, Nina," Miss Adaline said, sounding a bit harried. "We don't have a lesson scheduled today, do we?"

"Nope," Nina replied. "I just came to check on Breezy. Maybe go for a short ride if he's up to it."

"Okay, have fun." As the instructor disappeared around the corner, Nina headed for her pony's stall.

When she arrived, Breezy was nibbling at a pile of hay. But he stepped to the door eagerly when he heard the rustle of the wrapping on the mint Nina had brought him.

"Hi, buddy," she said as the pony lipped the treat off her palm. "How's it going? Feeling more energetic today?"

She figured there was only one sure way to find out. She didn't bother with a saddle, instead just slipping on the pony's bridle and then leading him outside. It had been a while since she'd ridden bareback, but she always enjoyed it.

Breezy stood patiently by the outdoor mounting block while Nina vaulted onto his broad back. He flicked an ear back toward her when she gave a cluck and a squeeze to ask him to move off.

"Let's go for a walk, Breezy," she said, squeezing again. "Walk on!"

This time the pony obeyed, ambling off toward the trail leading out into the park. Did his walk feel extra slow, or did it just feel different because Nina wasn't used to riding bareback these days? She wasn't sure. So as soon as they reached a wide, flat spot on the trail, with no bicyclists or strollers in sight to get in the way, she asked for a trot.

This time there was no doubt—Breezy obeyed her request, but from the first stride he felt sluggish and uninspired. As soon as Nina stopped pushing him forward with her legs, he drifted to a halt.

"Oh, Breezy." Nina felt like crying as she leaned forward to rub his neck. "What's wrong with you? I wish you could just tell me!"

She slid down and looped the reins back over his head. Then she led him over to a green patch in a sunny clearing beside the trail. The pony dove eagerly for the grass, leading Nina around as he gobbled one tasty mouthful of blades after another.

Nina watched him graze. "Well, whatever's wrong with you, it doesn't seem to be affecting your appetite," she joked weakly. Then she bit her lip. What in the world was going on with her pony?

She let him graze for about half an hour, then led him back to the barn. On the way inside, she passed Miss Adaline again. The riding instructor was leading the stable's smallest school pony with a tiny child perched precariously in the saddle.

"Have a fun ride!" Nina told the little girl with a smile.

"Thanks!" The young rider beamed at her. "Giddy up, Sweetpea!"

"Easy, there." Miss Adaline kept a hand on the pony's bridle, even though Sweetpea was completely ignoring the tiny rider's orders. "Nina, you'd better not put that pony back in his stall until you groom that saddle mark off of him." She winked at the little girl on Sweetpea. "See? You're not the only one who sometimes forgets to brush your pony after a ride."

"Saddle mark?" Nina laughed uncertainly, wondering if Miss Adaline was joking. "I don't think so—I rode bareback today."

"Ooh! I want to try riding bareback!" The little girl was so excited that she dropped her reins, which slid halfway down Sweetpea's neck.

Miss Adaline picked them up and handed them back to the girl. "Okay, then I guess you forgot to groom him yesterday," she told Nina. "Either way, he's got a massive girth mark."

"Yesterday? But I groomed him from head to hoof after I rode yesterday." Nina turned and stared at Breezy. For the first time, she noticed that he did, indeed, have a spot of rumpled hair where the girth would go. But how had it gotten there? She was positive that she'd left him spotless the day before.

Miss Adaline shrugged. "I don't know what to tell you," she said. "I haven't used him, and I'm pretty sure nobody else would touch him without permission. Couldn't hurt to ask around though."

Nina nodded, more confused than ever. Breezy was

such a quiet, well-trained pony that Miss Adaline occasionally borrowed him to teach a beginner student. But she always checked with Nina first. Had one of the other instructors misunderstood their agreement and decided to give him a try?

Moments later Breezy was back in his stall. "Be back soon," Nina told him with a pat. "I'll groom that girth mark off you—right after I figure out how it got there."

That didn't turn out to be as easy as she'd hoped. Nina checked with the barn manager, several of the grooms, and one of the other instructors. But none of them knew anything about that girth mark. Nina even called Jordan, remembering that her brother had played a prank on her once and moved Breezy to another stall. Could he be messing with Nina again by messing with her pony? But Jordan assured her that Brett had been glued to some dumb new video game all weekend and hadn't been anywhere near the stables.

"I worked all afternoon yesterday," a groom named Manny told Nina when she talked to him, scratching his beard. "Got in first thing this morning for feeding, too. If anyone had been hanging around your pony, I would've seen it."

"Okay," Nina said. "But someone messed with him between yesterday afternoon and now, and it wasn't me. What time did you leave last night?"

"Hmm, must've been a little before eight, I think?" Manny shrugged. "I was the last one here, actually. So if anyone did take that pony of yours for a joyride, it must've been after I left."

"Thanks." Nina wandered off, feeling uneasy. Could someone have sneaked into the barn after dark and saddled up Breezy for a ride? It was a scary thought.

She returned to the pony's stall and gave him another good grooming. Just as she finished, she heard a familiar laugh in the aisle nearby.

"Edie?" she called in surprise, sticking her head out of the stall. "Hi! What are you doing here?"

"Hi, Nina." Edie sounded surprised too, as she straightened up from tickling one of the barn cats. She glanced up and down the aisle, then smiled and took a step toward Nina. "I'm surprised to be here too. I told my parents that you ride here, and they secretly set up a lesson for me." She laughed. "Aren't they sneaky?"

"Awesomely sneaky." Nina let herself out of the stall. "Which horse are you riding? I can help you get ready if you want—you know, show you where everything is."

"Um, thanks. I'm riding a pony called Simba. The manager said my instructor is teaching a lesson right now but she'll be done soon, so if you don't have time to help . . ."

"No, it's totally fine." Was it Nina's imagination, or was Edie sounding a little more formal than usual—almost standoffish? But she shrugged off the thought, figuring that Edie was probably just nervous about her first ride at a new place. "Simba's stall is this way—come on."

Soon Simba, a friendly Haflinger cross, was parked in the cross-ties. Nina showed Edie to the tack room and helped her find grooming tools. They chatted about school and other topics as they worked, though Nina couldn't help noticing that the new girl still didn't seem quite as open and friendly as she had before.

Finally, when she straightened up from Simba's hoof to

find Edie shooting her an odd look, Nina could no longer ignore the feeling that something was different between them. She already had one friend keeping her guessing about how she was feeling—she wasn't about to let that kind of situation get started with her new friend.

"Is everything okay with you?" she asked Edie bluntly. "No offense, but you're acting a little funny."

"What?" Edie let out a high-pitched peal of laughter. "No, I'm fine! Here, let me do his other feet."

She grabbed the hoof pick and hurried around to the other side of the horse. Nina followed.

"No, I'm serious," she said. "Did I say something to make you mad or what? Because if I did, I'm sorry. Just be honest with me, okay? Seriously, I can take it—tell me what I did wrong."

Edie stared at her for a moment, then sighed. "It's just—I heard something at school today," she said softly. "I didn't really believe it, at least I didn't want to, but . . ."

Nina shook her head, confused. "What do you mean? What did you hear? Something about me?"

"Yeah." Edie played with the hoof pick, not quite

meeting Nina's gaze. "Some girls were talking to one another in the restroom, saying they heard you're, um . . ."

"I'm what?" Nina said. "Too talkative? Weird and pushy? That I smell like a horse?"

Edie looked surprised, and then laughed at the last one. "Not that," she said. "I wouldn't mind that at all."

"What, then?" Nina pressed. "What were they saying?"

"Um . . ." Edie glanced around, clearly not wanting to be overheard. "I guess someone told one of them that you're, uh, a kleptomaniac who just got caught stealing stuff out of people's lockers."

"What?" Nina squawked so loudly that Simba jumped and eyed her suspiciously. "Who told them that?"

"I don't know." Edie shrugged. "Like I said, I only overheard them—I don't even know those girls. They looked like they're probably younger than us."

Nina clenched her fists, annoyed. She was used to the way gossip could spread like wildfire through such a small, tight-knit school. But she'd never had such a hateful rumor aimed at her before.

"It's not true, obviously," she told Edie. "I mean, you're

new—I get that you don't really know me or anyone else yet. But I swear to you, I've never stolen anything in my life." She paused and considered what she'd just said. "Actually, I take that back. When I was like four, I saw this pretty emerald ring I liked in a shop my mom's friend owns over on Magazine Street. Miss Marie was always so nice to me, I figured she wouldn't mind if I took it." She smiled at the memory. "But believe me, as soon as my mom found out what happened, she marched me right back there and made me return it and apologize. Then she and my dad spent the rest of the day explaining to me how stealing is wrong, even from a friend." She shot Edie a look. "Especially from a friend."

Edie nodded, looking relieved. "Okay, okay, I believe you," she said with a sheepish laugh. "I was kind of dubious to start with, to tell you the truth. I mean, I've had to make new friends at enough new schools that I've learned how to size people up pretty quickly, and I had such a good feeling about you." She shook her head. "I just worried for a moment there that I was losing my touch, I guess."

"Don't worry, you aren't," Nina assured her, glad that at least one problem in her life had been so easy to solve. "Now come on, let's finish getting this pony ready. Miss Adaline doesn't take kindly to tardiness."

• CHAPTER •
6

"BREEZY BOY, I'M SO GLAD YOU'RE BACK!" Nina gave her pony a big hug as soon as she dismounted after her lesson on Tuesday. She'd been worried all day that he'd be tired again after another weirdo secret midnight ride. But she'd examined him carefully while tacking up, and there were no signs of saddle marks. And as soon as she asked him to trot the first time, she could tell she had her old pony back—lazy, but not *too* lazy.

Jordan giggled as she hopped down from Freckles's saddle. "I guess his secret rider must've heard you were onto them, huh?"

"Maybe so," Miss Adaline said, stepping around to help

Jordan by running up her right-side stirrup. "I did some asking around too, but nobody seems to know anything."

"Well, I don't even care who it was or why they did it," Nina said. "Just as long as they've stopped."

That wasn't entirely true. She was still troubled by the thought that someone could just take her pony out for a ride with nobody knowing. What if Breezy had been hurt? Or worse yet, what if his secret rider never brought him back? She couldn't blame whoever it was for falling in love with such a fantastic pony. . . .

She was still thinking about that a few minutes later as she and Jordan groomed their ponies. "So, weird about Leah, huh?" Jordan said, breaking into Nina's thoughts.

Nina blinked at her, her mind immediately switching from one worrisome situation to the other. "Yeah."

Leah hadn't shown up for the day's lesson. This time, however, Miss Adaline had already known she wasn't coming. She'd told Nina and Jordan that Leah's mother had called that morning and said that Leah had to drop out of lessons for a while.

"So why would she give up lessons?" Jordan went on.

"Do you think it's what we were talking about before?"

"You mean about her being sick—*really* sick?" Nina shuddered. "I hope not."

Jordan pulled out her cell phone. "What diseases can kids our age get?" she said. "I'll do a search."

"Don't do that," Nina said quickly, but it was too late. Jordan's eyes went wide as she scanned her phone's screen. "What?" Nina couldn't help asking. "Did you find something?"

"Lots of stuff." Jordan bit her lip. "Like swine flu, and asthma, and meningitis—yikes, I don't really even know what that is, but it sounds bad! And of course . . ." She paused and swallowed hard. "Cancer."

"I'm sure she doesn't have cancer." Nina grabbed the phone and turned off the search. "Anyway, we're not going to figure out what's wrong with Leah by trolling the Internet for horrible diseases and stuff. We'll just have to wait until she feels like sharing."

She just hoped that would happen soon.

Later, Nina flopped on her bed with her laptop and pulled up the Pony Post. While she waited for the site to load, her mind wandered back to Leah. But she pushed that thought aside, focusing instead on the Expo. Whatever Leah decided, Nina still had that third ticket to give away. Who should she give it to? Her closest friend? That would probably be Trinity, but she was pretty sure Trinity wouldn't be that interested in spending a whole day looking at horses.

No, it made much more sense to give it to her horsiest friend. Other than Jordan and Leah, who would that be? One of the other girls from the barn? Jayla from the neighborhood, who sometimes came trail riding in the summer? Cousin Tommy's six-year-old daughter, Annie, who brought her stuffed unicorn with her everywhere she went? Then Nina thought of another option—what about Edie?

Thinking about Edie reminded Nina of the rumor the new girl had told her about. She picked at her bedspread, freaked out anew by the memory of what Edie had said. Who could be telling people nasty lies about Nina—and why?

She shook off those thoughts as she realized the Pony Post was waiting for her. Nina wasn't the type to waste a lot of time worrying over things she couldn't fix. Why stress over some dumb thing those younger girls had said about her? Her real friends would know that the stupid rumor wasn't even close to true. Even Edie had been quick to believe Nina, and they'd only known each other for a few days.

That thought made Nina feel better. She pulled the laptop closer and scanned the latest entries from her friends.

[BROOKE] Hi, all! Guess what? The new fly mask I ordered for Foxy finally got here!!! It's still rainy here so there aren't rly many flies yet, but I tried it on her and she looks supercute. I'll post a pic in a sec.

Right below Brooke's entry was a photo of Foxy wearing a pink fly mask with silver stars printed on it. Nina smiled, then scanned down to the next post.

[MADDIE] ADORBS! Sooo glad it finally came, I know u ordered it like a month ago. Foxy looks like a superstar. I keep telling Ms. Emerson I'm going to get Cloudy one of those masks with big googly eyes printed on it, ha ha ha! (She keeps saying if I do, Cloudy might have to go into witness protection to get away from my craziness! Hahahahahahahahahaha!!!!!! ← crazy laugh)

[HALEY] Lol, Mads, u are too much! Brooke, the mask looks awesome. Foxy should totally be a horsey catalog model looking so good! Poor Wings will prolly have to settle for his regular old boring gray fly mask he already has, b/c I'm saving up for a new dressage girth.

[MADDIE] Cool! So did either of u ride today?

There were a few more posts after that, but Nina only scanned them. For some reason, she couldn't help feeling a little annoyed. Sure, Foxy looked awfully cute in her new fly mask. But was it fair that the other Pony Posters were making such a fuss over something like that, when they'd barely commented on her own big news about the Expo?

Immediately feeling guilty for those sorts of thoughts, Nina told herself she was being petty. Maybe her cousin was right and she'd bragged too much. Or maybe the other girls just hadn't realized how important the news was to Nina. Either way, maybe she should get over herself and post about it again—maybe ask their advice about who to invite with that third ticket.

But when she heard her mother calling her name, Nina couldn't help a flash of relief as she clicked off the site and hurried to see what she wanted.

"Oh no," Nina exclaimed aloud as soon as she asked Breezy for a trot on Wednesday afternoon. "Don't tell me . . ."

She gave the pony another kick. They were out for a trail ride, but had barely made it past the stable gates. At her second request, Breezy shook his head irritably and trotted for a few strides before dropping back to a choppy walk.

"Seriously?" Nina muttered with a sigh. She'd checked the pony carefully for saddle marks, but hadn't seen a hair out of place. That had made her hope that those secret midnight rides really were over.

But now it seemed they might not be. Had someone sneaked in again last night to take her pony for a joyride?

She sighed again. "Come on, Breezy," she said, turning him around. "Let's go back."

"So on Wednesday I was pretty sure someone had ridden him," Nina told Edie. It was Friday, and the two girls were walking to their lockers before lunch period.

"Did you try riding yesterday?" Edie asked.

Nina nodded. "We just did a short trail ride," she said. "It was really hot, so we didn't do much. But he actually felt more like his normal self again."

"So you don't think anyone took him riding on Wednesday night?" Edie shivered. "It's so crazy that someone could just borrow your pony without permission like that!"

"Tell me about it," Nina said with feeling. "I'm definitely going out this afternoon to check on him. I just hope he's okay for my lesson tomorrow morning." She brightened. "By the way, I meant to ask if you maybe wanted to come out to the barn tomorrow? You didn't really get to meet Breezy when you had your lesson the other day, so I was thinking you could watch me and Jordan ride, and then come for a walk with us on the levee."

"That sounds great!" Edie said immediately. "I'm sure my parents will say yes. They love that I'm into riding, since it helps me meet people whenever we move." She giggled. "My dad also hopes that my interest in horses will keep me away from boys!"

Nina chuckled, but she was a little distracted. Leah had just stalked into view at the end of the hall, every inch of her expression and body language sending out prickly vibes. She'd been keeping to herself all week, pretty much refusing to talk to Nina or their other friends.

But that wasn't the only weird thing going on that week. More rumors about Nina had been going around school lately. Edie, Trinity, and other friends had filled her in on some of them—like the one about how Nina had been born with a tail, or the one that she ate cat food as an after-school snack . . .

None of the rumors were as bad as that first one. Still, Nina didn't like being the subject of gossip—especially since most of it was so ridiculous. Who could be spreading such mean stories about her?

She'd done her best to forget about that by the time she walked into the stable after school. But all it took was one look at Breezy to put her in a bad mood again.

"No way!" she blurted out, letting herself into his stall and running her fingers over his back, where a saddle mark was clearly visible.

Breezy nudged her, looking for a treat. Nina pulled a mint out of her pocket and fed it to him, but she barely felt him slobbering on her palm. She was frowning, tempted to storm out of the stall and demand answers about who was borrowing her pony without permission.

But what good would that do? She'd already asked everyone at the barn. If anyone knew anything about Breezy's midnight rider, they weren't saying.

"It could be anyone," Nina muttered, running her fingers through Breezy's tangled forelock. "It's not like this stable is Fort Knox." She smiled as the pony nosed at her, clearly hoping for another mint. "And I can't really blame whoever it is for choosing the cutest pony in the entire state of Louisiana, right?"

Her smile faded quickly and she sighed, feeling out of sorts. First there was the mysterious situation with Breezy, then one of her best friends had turned into a cranky grump who wouldn't tell anyone what was wrong, and now there were these stupid rumors. . . . Nina hated feeling frustrated and helpless about so many things in her life all at once.

"So let's do something about it," she muttered, quoting one of her aunt Iris's favorite comments.

There didn't seem to be much she could do about the rumors other than wait for them to pass, so she turned her attention to Leah. Whatever was going on with her, it was clearly making her miserable. And friends didn't let friends deal with bad stuff on their own, right? Even if she really did have some terrible disease, Nina wanted to help in any way she could. But she could only do that if Leah told her what was wrong.

"And if she doesn't want to come to me, I'll just have to go to her," Nina told Breezy, fishing another mint out of her pocket. "Whether she likes it or not."

As the pony eagerly gobbled the treat, Nina checked her watch. She wouldn't have enough time to make it over to Leah's house and still make it home in time for Friday family dinner. But she could go over there right after her lesson tomorrow.

"It's a plan," she told Breezy with a smile. "I'll just show up at her door and refuse to leave until she tells me what's wrong. And that's that."

· CHAPTER ·
7

NINA FELT A LITTLE BETTER AS SOON AS
she had a plan to deal with the Leah situation. Now it was
time to do something about Breezy's nighttime visitor.

"Be right back," she told the pony as she let herself out
of the stall.

She hurried down the aisle and around the corner to
the stable office. Nobody was there, so she poked her head
into the feed room. The barn manager, a tall, lean, brisk
woman with a deep tan and short brown hair, was scoop-
ing feed into buckets for the horses' dinner.

"Hi, Nina," the manager said. "What can I do for
you?"

Nina told her about the latest saddle mark. "Isn't there any way to figure out who's sneaking in and riding him?" she finished. "Otherwise I'm afraid they'll never stop!"

The manager sighed and dropped her scoop into the feed bin. "Not without hiring a nighttime guard, and we can't afford that," she said. "Sorry, Nina. If someone really is sneaking in at night to ride your pony—"

"Someone definitely is!" Nina broke in, a little surprised that the manager didn't seem fully convinced. "You should see Breezy—he's so tired these days he can hardly move when I try to ride him."

"Hmm." The manager reached for another bucket. "Yes, Adaline did say something about that. . . . Well, maybe I can ask around and see if I can find someone with a motion-activated security camera we could borrow for a few days. Maybe if we set it up near his stall we'll catch the pony rustler that way."

Nina brightened. "That sounds great!" she exclaimed. "How soon do you think you can find a camera like that?"

The manager shrugged. "I'll try to remember to send

some emails this weekend. I'll let you know how it goes when I hear back from people."

"Oh, okay." Nina was tempted to urge her to work faster, but she bit her tongue and kept quiet. The manager didn't seem to think this problem was very urgent. But at least she was willing to do something. Unless Nina came up with a better plan, she would just have to try to be patient. Not that that was going to be easy. . . .

That night, Uncle Oscar and Aunt Lou were hosting Friday night's family dinner. They lived in a rambling old camelback Victorian in Bywater, and there was plenty of room for everyone around their big oak dining table. Aunt Toni and Uncle Elijah were away visiting friends in Alabama, and Cousin DeeDee's boyfriend was off on a fishing trip with his buddies, but everyone else was there, even Nina's ninety-six-year-old great-aunt Shirley, for a total of twenty adults and ten kids. As usual, Nina was the only one between the ages of seven and thirty, but that was normal for her. She loved being able to go back and forth from playing tag with the younger kids or tickling Cousin

Charlotte's pudgy, cheerful one-year-old daughter, Ella, to discussing interesting topics with the grown-ups.

Tonight, though, Nina was a little distracted. She barely heard the discussion of local politics as she played with her food.

Finally Uncle Oscar leaned over and poked her on the shoulder. "Wake up, Nina Beanie!" he boomed, using his favorite pet name for her. "Are we putting you to sleep?"

Nina blinked, then smiled. "Sorry, guys," she said. "I guess I'm just a little distracted."

"Ah." Oscar leaned back and winked broadly at the others. "Boy trouble, eh?"

"No!" Nina said quickly, which made all the adults laugh. Rolling her eyes, she added, "Pony trouble, actually."

"What's wrong, child?" Aunt Vi helped herself to more Brussels sprouts. "Did you and that little pony of yours forget how to win blue ribbons at your horse shows?"

"No, it's not that. . . ." Nina launched into the whole story, telling her relatives about Breezy's mystery rider. Her parents had already heard all about it, of course, but the others listened with interest.

"Wow," Cousin Jeremy's wife, Becks, said when Nina had finished. "That's wild. A secret midnight rider, huh?"

"Sounds like the Wild West, not civilized New Orleans," Gramma Rose commented, adding a quiet "tut tut" after she said it.

"I know, it's crazy," Nina said, idly pushing a piece of chicken around on her plate. "But the manager says she can't afford to hire a security guard, so—"

"So what's the problem?" her cousin Charlotte said jokingly. "You can just do a stakeout yourself! Isn't that your dream come true, moving right into that barn with your pony?"

Several of the others chuckled. But Cousin DeeDee, an outspoken thirty-one-year-old with a sharp chin and a short Afro, looked thoughtful. "You know, that could actually work," she said. "I mean, whoever's sneaking rides on Breezy obviously knows there's nobody there at night, so it should be easy to catch him or her."

Aunt Vi looked alarmed. "Our Nina, sleeping over in a dark barn in the middle of Audubon Park?" she exclaimed. "Sounds downright dangerous to me!"

"I agree," Gramma Rose said.

But Nina was already excited. This could be the answer! Why hadn't she thought of it herself? "No, DeeDee's right," she cried. "It's the easiest way to find out for sure who's doing it!"

"I'll go with her," DeeDee added before anyone else could protest further. "It'll be fun—like a slumber party."

"Are you really that bored with Tim out of town?" Aunt Iris asked with a chuckle and a wink at DeeDee's mother, Lou.

DeeDee ignored her. "What do you say?" she said to Nina. "Want to give it a try? We could do it tonight if you want."

"Sure!" Nina said eagerly. Then she cleared her throat and glanced at her parents. "I mean, can we—please?"

Her mother and father traded a look. "I don't know . . . ," her mother began.

"Oh, let them do it," Kim spoke up. "Why not? They'll have their phones, and it's not like some axe murderer is likely to be sneaking in to ride a pony."

"We'll be careful," DeeDee added. "Cross our hearts. Right, Nina?"

Nina drew an *X* over her chest with one finger. "Promise!" she said. "Please, guys? I really, really want to find out who's sneaking rides on Breezy, and the manager isn't even sure when she might be able to find a camera, and what if something happens and Breezy turns up lame, or maybe disappears entirely? If that happened, I'd just—"

"Okay, okay, you've talked us into it!" Her father held up both hands in surrender. "I know we'd never hear the end of it if anything happened to that pony."

"Hmm." Uncle Oscar sounded disapproving as he stared at Nina and DeeDee. "This seems like a foolish idea to me."

"Color TV seemed like a foolish idea to you, Pop," Cousin Jeremy said with a chuckle. "The girls are sensible enough not to get themselves in trouble."

"I hope so." Nina's mother still sounded dubious. She looked at DeeDee. "You'll just watch, and not confront anybody, right? As soon as you see who's doing it, you can sneak away and alert the authorities."

"For sure," DeeDee said. "We'll just peek and maybe snap a photo as evidence, right, Nina?"

"You'll have to get permission from that barn manager first, though, of course," Nina's father put in. "There might not be time to reach her tonight."

"Sure there is." Nina was already reaching for her phone. "I'll send her a text right now. . . ."

Within minutes, permission had been granted. Some of the adults still seemed disapproving, but Nina's heart was pounding with excitement as she shoveled the rest of her dinner into her mouth, hardly tasting Aunt Lou's delicious red beans and rice. It was time to get to the bottom of this mystery—and tonight was the night!

"Here we are," DeeDee sang out as she expertly pulled her tiny car into a free spot on St. Charles. She cut the engine and grinned at Nina. "Ready for the sleepover?"

"Ready!" Nina hopped out of the car and hurried around to open the hatchback. She pulled out her backpack and slung it over her shoulder, then grabbed the worn old picnic blanket they'd brought.

DeeDee picked up her own bag, and then locked the car. The two of them had brought snacks, drinks, and a few other things along to make them more comfortable. It was already dark, but the moon and the streetlights lit their way as they hurried along the familiar paths toward the stable. It took a few minutes to get there, but Nina and DeeDee had discussed strategy and decided the extra walk was worth it. They didn't want to park in the stable's lot since that would alert the midnight rider that someone was around.

When the stable buildings came into view beyond a row of live oaks dripping with Spanish moss, Nina slowed her pace and glanced at her cousin, putting a finger to her lips. DeeDee smiled and mimicked a cartoonish tiptoe, which made Nina giggle. Active, fun-loving DeeDee had always been one of her favorite cousins. But she hadn't spent much time alone with DeeDee since her boyfriend, Tim, had come along a few years earlier. This was going to be fun!

All the horses were in their stalls, most of them still working on the piles of hay the grooms had given them before leaving for the night. The barn felt warm and cozy and sleepy.

"Where's your pony?" DeeDee whispered.

"Down this way." Nina led her cousin around the corner into the aisle where Breezy's stall was located. The pony poked his head out over the half door when he heard them coming, his ears pricked. Then he let out a loud whinny.

"Breezy, hush!" Nina exclaimed softly, hurrying forward to feed him a treat. "We're supposed to be stealthy here, buddy!"

Behind her, she heard DeeDee snorting with laughter. "Yeah, we're ready for the secret service, all right," she said. "Come on, let's find a spot to wait where your noisy pony can't see us."

Nina had already thought about this part, deciding that the best place to stake out Breezy's stall was the empty stall across the aisle. They would be able to pull the half door most of the way shut, so they could peek out but not be easily spotted by anyone entering the aisle.

"It doesn't matter if Breezy can see us or not, though," she informed her cousin as they spread their blanket on the stall floor. "Horses have excellent senses of hearing and smell. He'll still know we're here."

"Okay." DeeDee flopped onto the blanket. "Then tell him to keep quiet, or this whole crazy scheme won't work."

"Crazy scheme?" Nina said with a grin. "Hey, it was your idea!"

"Who ever said I wasn't crazy?" DeeDee retorted, making Nina giggle. "Now toss me a root beer, would you? And let's bust open those cheese puffs too. . . ."

For a while after that, Nina and DeeDee stayed busy talking, eating, and slapping mosquitoes. The only other sounds came from the horses moving around in their stalls, the occasional bark of a dog, and the distant buzz of traffic outside the park.

Nina was telling DeeDee about Leah's recent weird behavior when she stopped suddenly, cocking her head at a new sound. "What was that?" she whispered.

"What—this?" DeeDee imitated the sound Nina had just heard, a hoarse *hoo-hoo-hoo-hoo*. "That's not your midnight rider. It's just a barred owl."

"How'd you know that?" Nina asked, impressed.

DeeDee shrugged. "I know everything." She grinned. "Actually, I remember it from some nature walk I did with the church youth group in City Park as a kid."

Nina shivered as the sound came again. "It's kind of spooky, isn't it?"

DeeDee made ghostly fingers at her. "Yes. Are you afraid it's an omen that Great-Aunt Serena's ghost is coming for yoooooooou?" she whispered in a dramatic voice.

"Stop it!" Nina giggled and pushed her cousin's hands away. "You know Serena and I are friends now."

She smiled, thinking back to the previous autumn, when she'd feared that the ghost of a Civil-War-era ancestor was haunting her. Even then, Nina had known that there was no such thing as a ghost. Still, on a night like tonight, in the darkened barn with spooky shadows on the walls and an owl hooting in the trees outside, it was a little easier to believe. . . .

"Okay." DeeDee settled back, cracking open another root beer. "But did anyone ever tell you the story about the time Gramma Rose swore that Great-Aunt Serena was stealing her socks from the clothesline?"

After that, they swapped old family stories for a while, mostly of the ghostly variety. By the time they ran out of tales, Nina's eyelids were growing heavy and she was yawning every few seconds. The moon had set, and it was dark and a little muggy in the stall.

"What time is it, anyway?" she murmured, wiggling around to find a more comfortable position on the hard ground.

DeeDee turned on her phone, the soft glow casting crazy shadows everywhere. "Almost midnight," she said. "Want to pack it in? Looks like your secret rider might not be coming tonight after all."

"Yeah, you may be right. I—" Suddenly Nina sat up at a sound from outside—and this time it wasn't an owl. "Shh! Did you hear that?"

"Serena? Is that you?" DeeDee whispered back jokingly. Then her eyes went wide. "Hold it, I do hear something! Footsteps—and they're coming this way!"

She crawled to the cracked-open door and peeked out. Nina shoved in, peering out as well. The footsteps were louder now, crunching on the gravel outside the barn's main entrance. Then came the sound of the big sliding door creaking open, followed by more footsteps, quick and light and hurried. . . .

Nina held her breath, waiting for whoever it was to turn the corner and come into sight. She could see that DeeDee was holding her phone, ready to snap a photo, although she wasn't sure it do any good without a flash. . . .

She leaned forward, straining her eyes against the dark as a figure came into view. But it was impossible to see much, other than that whoever it was wasn't much bigger than Nina herself. Gritting her teeth, Nina willed her eyes to cut through the darkness like a cat, or an owl, or even a horse. . . .

The figure opened Breezy's stall door, and the pony stepped toward her. As the figure led the pony out, Nina leaned closer to her cousin.

"We have to do something!" she hissed directly into DeeDee's ear. "We can't just let her—"

Then she gasped as the person leading her pony stepped into a section of the aisle that was dimly illuminated by the safety lights just outside. Finally Nina got a good look at Breezy's midnight rider, and when she did, she immediately forgot all about being stealthy.

"You!" she blurted out, leaping to her feet and pushing out of the stall in one quick motion. "I can't believe it's *you*!"

· CHAPTER ·
8

NINA STARED AT THE PALE, VERY FAMILIAR face in front of her. Behind her, she heard her cousin step out of the stall. "Nina, careful . . . ," DeeDee began.

"It's okay. It's just Leah. My friend." Nina glared at Leah, who was clutching Breezy's lead rope as if it were a lifeline.

"N-Nina?" Leah blurted out, clearly startled.

"You're the one who's been riding Breezy at night?" Nina exclaimed. "I can't believe this!"

"What? No, it's not that." Leah cleared her throat, her pale eyes shifting this way and that. "It's just, um, I was at the barn today and I heard Breezy was acting kind of colicky. So I was in the neighborhood and decided to come check on him."

"You were in the neighborhood? At midnight?" Nina grabbed Breezy's lead rope out of Leah's hand and led the pony back into his stall, giving him a pat before unclipping the lead and closing the door. "Yeah, right. You live way over in the Marigny!"

"All right, young lady," DeeDee spoke up. She stepped over and flipped on a light switch nearby, causing both girls and most of the horses to blink at the sudden glare. "Why don't you tell us what you're really doing with Nina's pony?"

Leah glowered at DeeDee. "Who are you?" she demanded.

"The person who's asking you a question." It was amazing how stern fun-loving DeeDee could sound when she put on that tone of voice—she was almost as scary as an angry Aunt Lou. "So let's have an answer."

Leah stuck out her lower lip, narrowing her eyes at DeeDee and then glancing at Nina. "Nothing," she muttered. "I mean, so what if I went for a little ride or two?"

"So you admit it?" Nina took a step toward her. "You've been riding Breezy at night?"

"Okay, yes, it was me!" Leah blurted out, her cheeks going red. "Now are you happy?"

"Not really." Now that Leah had admitted it, Nina's anger evaporated, replaced by bewilderment. "Why did you do it? I mean, I always said you could ride Breezy anytime you wanted."

"Yeah. So that's what I was doing." Leah smirked. "See? So what's the big deal?"

DeeDee cleared her throat, looking annoyed. Nina could understand why—Leah was acting pretty rude. But she shot her cousin a be-quiet look, hoping DeeDee could read it. Nina knew Leah well enough to know that yelling at her probably wasn't going to get them anywhere. That would just make Leah defensive and cause her to shut down.

"Just tell me why—please?" Nina said to Leah. "I really don't understand why you've been doing this, and not even saying anything to me about it."

"Yeah, well, maybe I was afraid to talk to you." Leah

was still smirking. "I mean, from what I hear around school, you're a total klepto with a tail who eats cat food, right? Who wants to talk to someone like that?"

Nina narrowed her eyes at Leah. "Wait," she said. "I get it. That was you too, wasn't it?"

"What was her?" DeeDee put in. "What's she talking about with the cat food stuff, Nina?"

Nina didn't take her eyes off Leah as she answered her cousin. "Somebody's been spreading all kinds of mean rumors about me at school this week. And I think I just figured out who it was."

Leah returned her glare. "What do you care about a few silly rumors? I thought you didn't pay attention to what anyone thinks of you," she spat out. "In fact, I figured you'd love being the center of attention. Isn't that why you wear all those weird old clothes and stuff?"

Nina shook her head. "Whatever. This isn't about my clothes, okay? Just tell me why you've been spreading all those lies about me." She was more perplexed than ever by her friend's behavior. "Seriously, Leah. Did I do something to make you mad?"

"Duh, not everything is all about you, Nina." Leah rolled her eyes. "Don't be so self-centered, okay? Now get out of my way, I have to go."

She started forward, clearly expecting Nina to step out of her way. But Nina wasn't going to step aside—or back down. Not this time. She was usually pretty laid back, but Leah had pushed her to her limit.

"Stop." She stepped forward, preventing Leah from getting past. "You're not going anywhere. Not until you tell me what's really going on with you—with us." She stared at her friend, though Leah wouldn't quite meet her gaze. "We've been friends for a long time. You owe me that much, at least."

"Friends?" DeeDee muttered behind Nina. "That's what you call this?"

"Yeah." Nina glanced over her shoulder at her cousin. "Friends. Ever since we met in first grade, and Leah shared her cookie with me after mine fell on the floor."

When she returned her gaze to her friend, she saw that Leah's lower lip was trembling. Nina took a step toward her.

"Leah?" she said, suddenly concerned. Leah might complain a lot, but she hardly ever cried. "What is it? Seriously, you can tell me—no matter what it is."

Leah let out one loud sniffle, and then burst into tears. "I—I can't!" she wailed. "I can't tell anyone about this."

Nina hurried forward, enveloping her friend in a hug. Leah tried to pull away, but when Nina tightened her grip she suddenly shuddered and collapsed against her.

"No, really," Leah mumbled into Nina's shoulder, her tears already soaking her shirt. "It's something really terrible."

"You can trust me," Nina said, stroking her back. "With anything."

"Not with this," Leah insisted with a sniffle. "I mean, don't you get it? Why else do you think I've been avoiding everyone all week—especially you? That's why I started those rumors, because I figured it would keep you busy and stop you from harassing me about stuff. . . ."

"But what is it?" Nina clutched her friend more tightly, suddenly recalling her talks with Jordan. "Is it—are you sick? I mean, really sick? Like a disease?"

"Huh?" Leah blinked. "No! Nothing like that, duh. I mean, I really can't . . ."

Her voice trailed off, and she looked at something over Nina's shoulder. A second later DeeDee cleared her throat.

"Maybe I'll just step outside for some air," Nina's cousin said. "Leave you two girls alone to talk."

"Okay." Nina shot DeeDee a grateful look, realizing that her cousin had just figured out that Leah might not be comfortable talking about whatever it was in front of her. "I'll let you know when we're done."

"Fine. Call me if you need me."

She hurried off. Leah pushed away from Nina, wandering over to collapse onto the little bench against the wall where Nina usually set her grooming tote. Nina followed, perching beside her.

"So?" she said quietly. "Will you tell me now?"

Leah took a deep, shaky breath and shot Nina a sidelong look. "Remember that phone call I got from my mom after our lesson?"

Nina nodded, immediately remembering how Leah had rushed off after that call. "Yeah."

"Well, when I got home both my parents were waiting for me." Leah picked at her cuticle, not looking at Nina now. "It turned out they had terrible news they wanted to tell me in person. We're broke!"

"Huh?" At first Nina didn't understand what she meant. "Broke what?"

"Broke! As in no money, poor, broke."

"What? How?"

"I don't know, I don't really understand all the dumb details." Leah shrugged and kicked at a stray strand of hay on the stable floor. "But my dad's business partner did something sneaky and, like, totally illegal, and then skipped town. All our money's tied up in it, pretty much. Plus Dad might go to jail if they can't find his partner. . . ."

Her lip was quivering again. Nina scooted closer, then slung an arm around her for another hug. "I'm sorry," she said. "That's horrible."

"I know, right?" Leah took a deep breath, clearly fighting back more tears. "Anyway, that's why I had to drop out of lessons. We have, like, no money. Not even for groceries or whatever." She shrugged. "The only reason they didn't pull me out of our school yet is because they already prepaid tuition for the whole year. Next year's another story. . . ."

Nina was horrified. She was rarely at a loss for words, but this time she wasn't sure what to say to make her friend feel better. "I can't believe you've been dealing with this all on your own," she managed at last. "What can I do to help?"

"Nothing," Leah said immediately, her voice going hard and wary again. "You can't do anything. And you'd better not tell anyone else about this, or else! I mean it, Nina—*nobody*!"

"But I'm sure other people would—" Nina began.

"No!" Leah shot up from her place on the bench, glaring down at Nina with her fists clenched at her sides. "You have to swear to me you won't breathe a word! Not to your friend out there—" She waved a hand in the general direction DeeDee had disappeared. "Not to people at school. Not to your parents. Nobody, okay?"

"Okay, okay." Nina stood up too. "I promise. But only

if you promise me that you'll only ride Breezy in the day-time from now on, and maybe try not to tire him out quite as much, either."

"Huh?" Leah blinked at her, clearly taken by surprise by the sudden change in topic. "Breezy?"

"Yeah, you know that cute little pony you've been sneaking rides on?" Nina stepped over to pat Breezy, who was hanging his head out into the aisle watching them. "I know it must be killing you not to be able to ride. So you can keep riding him if you want."

"Really?" Leah stared from Nina to Breezy and back again, as if not daring to believe her ears.

"Yeah. How about tomorrow?" Nina offered. "You can take my spot in our lesson." Then she remembered something. "Oh, wait—except that's when I invited Edie to come watch. Well, that's okay, though, she probably won't care if—"

"Forget it," Leah interrupted. "I'm definitely not rid-ing in our regular lesson. Jordan's supernosy; she'll guess something's going on, and I just don't want to deal with it. And that new girl, Edie, talks way too much; if she finds out the whole school will know before long."

Nina didn't think that was particularly fair—as far as she knew, Leah had barely spoken to Edie and had no grounds to accuse her of being a gossip. Under the circumstances, though, she figured it wasn't worth arguing about.

"Okay, okay," Nina said. "Forget tomorrow, then. How about Sunday?"

"I don't know." Leah frowned, kicking at the floor. "It's not like I can exactly plan my life right now, okay? I'll have to let you know."

She was starting to sound cranky again. Nina nodded. "Okay."

"Just remember—you promised not to tell, right?" Leah demanded. "You swore you wouldn't say anything to anyone!"

"Yeah, that's right." Nina smiled. "You can trust me, Leah. It'll be okay."

Leah just shrugged at that. "I have to go," she muttered. Pausing only long enough to give Breezy a brief rub on the nose, she rushed for the exit.

Nina watched her go, feeling worried. A moment later her cousin came in.

"I saw your friend run past," DeeDee said. "Are you sure she'll be okay by herself at this hour?"

Nina hadn't really thought about that. Normally she would have assumed that Leah might have called a cab to get home at this time of night. Now that she was poor, she probably didn't have that option and would have to walk or take the bus. But it was too late to stop her now.

"I'm sure she'll be fine," Nina said, as much to reassure herself as DeeDee. "We can go home now."

As they crouched down to gather their things from the empty stall, DeeDee shot her a curious look. "Are you going to tell me what that was all about?"

"I can't." Nina sat back on her heels and glanced at her cousin. "I wish I could, I really do. But I promised Leah I wouldn't tell anyone what she just told me."

"Okay." DeeDee nodded. "Can you at least tell me she's not in any bodily danger? Nobody's beating her up, or anything like that?"

"No!" Nina's eyes widened. "No way. It's definitely nothing like that."

"Good." DeeDee sounded relieved. "Okay, let's feed the rest of these corn chips to that endless pit of a pony of yours, and then we can get out of here. I'm bushed."

"Yeah." Nina walked over to give Breezy a pat, suddenly aware of just how exhausted she was. "Me too."

· CHAPTER ·
9

NINA GROANED AS SHE FELT A SOFT PAW PAT
her on the cheek. Cracking one eye open, she found
Teniers staring back at her with his vivid blue Siamese
eyes. The room was filled with bright sunlight, telling her
she'd slept very late.

"Curse cats who taught themselves how to open
doors," Nina grumbled, opening her other eye as Bastet
leaped onto the bed too, immediately attacking Nina's
elbow under the sheets. She pushed the cats aside and
sat up, stretching and yawning. Then she glanced at the
clock.

"Only a little more than an hour until I have to be

at the barn for my lesson," she told the cats. "Guess I'd better get up. . . ."

She crawled out of bed and grabbed her robe. Then she noticed her laptop lying on the desk where she'd dropped it the evening before. She and DeeDee had stopped at the house right after dinner to pick up the snacks and picnic blanket. While DeeDee was raiding the pantry, Nina had hurried to her room to grab a sweater in case it got chilly. While she was there, she'd briefly logged on to the Pony Post to give them a quick update on the stakeout.

Yawning again, she flipped open the computer and turned it on. Soon she was on the site. All three of her friends had left responses to her last post.

[HALEY] O gosh, Nina! A stakeout? That sounds so, I don't know, like a TV show or something! I hope ur careful!!!!

[BROOKE] Yes, I can't even imagine hiding out in the middle of New Orleans in the middle of the

night like that, waiting for who knows who!! Then
again, I can't imagine living in a big city like that in
the first place, lol, so what do I know? But I agree
with H—pls be careful!

[MADDIE] You guys worry too much. I always knew
Neens was a super secret agent ninja superhero
type. She'll be fine. N, just make sure you get back
here asap and let us know who u catch stealing
rides on Breezy Boy!!!!!!!!!

Nina read over the messages a second time, smiling
at Maddie's comments and wondering what to do. Leah
had sworn her to secrecy, and so far Nina had stuck to
that. She hadn't told DeeDee about Leah's news, and she
hadn't told her parents, either, when she got home last
night. They'd understood, since they knew Leah and they
trusted Nina. But how was Nina supposed to explain all
this to the Pony Post? If she told them she'd found out her
friend was Breezy's secret rider, they'd want to know why.
She didn't want to break Leah's trust, but she also didn't

want to lie to her other friends—or keep secrets from them, either. She almost wished she hadn't told the Pony Post about the stakeout in the first place.

But she took back that thought immediately. It was already weird enough not really discussing the Expo with her online friends. No way did she want to add something else to the list!

Besides, Leah herself always referred to the Pony Posters as Nina's imaginary friends, right? So what was the harm in spilling Leah's secret to people she considered imaginary? She could no more get mad about that than if Nina whispered the news to her battered old stuffed penguin. . . .

"It's not like any of them will ever even meet Leah in person, right?" she murmured to Teniers, who head butted her arm in response.

Nina decided to take that as a yes. Opening a new text box, she started typing before she could second-guess herself. She poured out the whole story, along with her worries about what would happen to Leah and her family now.

As soon as she hit send, she logged off and set the

computer aside. She would have to hurry if she wanted to shower and eat something before it was time to head to the barn.

"Go, Breezy!" Jordan cheered as Nina and her pony cleared the last of a small course of jumps that Miss Adaline had set up as the final exercise of the day. "I guess his secret rider didn't wear him out last night, huh?"

"Guess not." Nina tried to sound light and casual. She hadn't breathed a word about last night's adventures to Jordan, Miss Adaline, or Edie, who was watching the lesson from her perch on the ring fence. But it was obvious to everyone that the Chincoteague pony was feeling lively that day.

Nina gave Breezy a pat as she pulled up next to Jordan. Freckles had already taken his turn over the course, so Miss Adaline clapped her hands.

"Okay, let's let them quit there," she said. "Good work, girls. Walk around the ring a few times to cool out, and I'll see you next time."

With a little wave, she hurried out of the ring to prepare for her next lesson. Edie hopped down from the fence, hurrying over to walk between the two ponies as their riders steered them around the ring.

"That was great," she said, patting one pony and then the other. "Miss Adaline is a really good teacher, isn't she?"

"She's the best." Jordan smiled down at her. Nina had introduced the two of them when Edie had arrived at the barn, and they'd hit it off right away. Then again, Nina was starting to realize that Edie had a talent for hitting it off with just about anyone. She supposed that was a skill you had to acquire when you moved around as much as Edie did.

"Hey, Edie," Nina said. "I talked to Miss Adaline before you got here, and she said it would be okay if you tried riding Breezy after the lesson. So what do you say? Want to take him for a little spin? Maybe you can finish cooling him out for me."

Edie gasped. "Are you kidding?" she exclaimed. "Thanks, Nina! That sounds amazing!"

Nina dismounted and unbuckled her helmet. "Here," she said, handing it to Edie. "This should fit you okay."

Nina strapped on the helmet, then followed as Nina led Breezy over to the mounting block. Soon she was in the saddle.

"Stirrups look a little long," Nina said. "Here, let me help you."

She fiddled with the left stirrup, moving it up two holes. When she looked up, she realized that Edie was already adjusting the other stirrup herself. Nina smiled, relieved to see that the other girl really did seem to know what she was doing in the saddle. That was good. She'd brought more than one friend to the stable who had claimed to be an experienced rider, only to discover once they were on Breezy's back that they'd only been on a vacation trail ride or two and really didn't know much at all.

Meanwhile, Jordan had finished walking Freckles the rest of the way around the ring. Now she rode over and dismounted near the gate.

"I wish I could stay and watch your ride," she told Edie. "But I promised my mom I'd come straight home today—we're supposed to take my grandma shopping and she gets grouchy if we're even half a second late."

"It's just as well," Edie said with a smile. "That way, if I fall off nobody will ever need to know."

Jordan laughed. "See you around, Edie. Bye, Neens."

"See you Tuesday," Nina said.

"Oh! No you won't, actually." Jordan shrugged. "I have a dentist's appointment, so I have to miss our next lesson."

"Oh. Well, see you around the neighborhood, then."

"For sure. Bye!"

As Jordan let herself and Freckles out of the ring, Nina checked Breezy's girth to make sure it hadn't loosened during the lesson. Then she stepped back and smiled at Edie.

"Okay, he's all yours," she said. "Let's see what you've got."

Edie turned out to be a decent rider. After a few minutes of walking, Nina suggested she try a little trot. Breezy stepped off into the faster gait as soon as Edie asked, and Edie transitioned smoothly into a rising trot.

"Nice!" Nina said when Edie brought the pony to a crisp halt in front of her a few minutes later. "You look good up there!"

"Thanks." Edie's cheeks were flushed with exertion and happiness. "My dad would say it runs in my blood."

"What do you mean?" Nina fell into step beside Breezy as Edie sent him into an ambling walk again to finish cooling out.

"I was named after my great-grandmother Edith," Edie explained, letting the reins slip through her fingers so Breezy could lower his head and relax. "She died way before I was born, but everyone tells me I look just like her. Anyway, she used to take the students from our school riding here in the park. It was, like, part of the curriculum I guess, at least it was when she first founded the place as a private school for young ladies way back in the day."

"Founded it?" For a second Nina didn't understand. "Wait—you mean your great-grandma founded our school? As in, started it?"

"Uh-huh." Edie shrugged. "You know the portrait hanging over the fireplace in the headmaster's office? That's Great-Grandmother Edith."

"Wow." Nina vaguely knew the portrait Edie meant, though she'd never paid much attention to it. Now she vowed to check it out more carefully the next chance she got. "I mean, I knew the school used to be all girls, and I knew it had been around awhile." She shook her head. "But I never knew riding used to be part of the deal! Too bad they stopped doing that."

"Yeah." Edie laughed. "Anyway, what about your family? Are they from New Orleans originally?"

"Not my mom," Nina said, reaching over to swish away a fly buzzing around Breezy's ears. "She grew up in New Jersey and went to art school up north too. She came down on vacation after she graduated, met my dad in a jazz club, and never went back."

"Really? That's so romantic!" Edie looked impressed.

"Yeah, I know, they're total saps." Nina giggled. "Anyway, my dad's side of the family has been in this city since at least the early 1800s, maybe longer. . . ." She went on to tell Edie more about her family's history, including the tales about Serena.

By the time they untacked Breezy together and started grooming him, they'd moved on to talking about Edie's travels. After that they moved on to other things—school, friends, and more. Eventually Nina even found herself telling Edie about the Pony Post.

"And ever since the site went live, all four of us post almost every day. Just stuff about our ponies, our lives, keeping in touch . . ." Nina shot Edie a slightly sheepish glance. "Go ahead, make fun of me for being so into it. Everybody else does."

"No way, not me." Edie ran a brush over Breezy's back. "Actually I belong to a similar site myself."

"You do?"

"Uh-huh." Edie dropped the brush back in Nina's tote. "It's me and a bunch of other expat kids I met while living overseas."

"Expat?" Nina echoed uncertainly. She'd heard the term before but wasn't sure what it meant.

"It's short for 'expatriate,'" Edie explained. "It means someone living in a country where they're not a citizen.

Anyway, being a diplomat's kid means meeting tons of cool people and then having to leave them behind when you move again. On the site, we can all keep in touch and keep track of where everyone's living and stuff like that."

"Cool." Nina smiled. "Sounds like your site probably has more than four members, huh?"

"Definitely." Edie giggled. "It's not as exclusive as the Pony Post, but it's still pretty great. Want to see?" She dug her phone out of her pocket.

Nina peered over her shoulder as Edie pulled up the site. After that, Nina showed Edie the Pony Post, scrolling through some of the photos her friends had posted of their ponies lately.

They were laughing over a shot of Maddie trying to do a handstand on Cloudy's back when Breezy suddenly nudged Nina in the side. She glanced at him.

"Oops," she said. "I think Breezy is tired of looking at websites. Want to help me take him for a walk on the levee now?"

Edie checked her watch. "I wish I could," she said.

"But I'm supposed to go to a party with my parents soon, and they'll kill me if I'm late. Maybe next time?"

"Sure." Nina was sure there would be a next time. That was partly because she could tell that Edie was a real horse lover, and partly because the new girl was already feeling like a real friend. "Hey," she added impulsively. "I just had an idea. Want to go the Big Easy Horse Expo with me next weekend?"

"The what?" Edie said.

Nina quickly explained. "So Jordan is coming, and probably Leah, too." She didn't bother to explain about the Leah situation. "The third ticket is yours if you want it."

"Really?" Edie gasped. "That sounds so amazing, Nina! A whole day of horses? How great is that? Thank you so much! I'll call home right now and get permission."

Nina finished picking out Breezy's hooves while Edie placed her call. She could tell even before the other girl hung up that it was good news.

"They said yes!" Edie sang out, doing a funny little dance step. "I'm so excited!"

"Me too!" Nina laughed and imitated the dance step. "It'll be a blast!"

After Edie left, Nina took Breezy out to graze, though she decided to stick to the grassy areas near the barn instead of walking all the way out to the levee. Talking about the Expo had reminded her of Leah and her problems.

"Not that I should have needed reminding," she murmured to her pony, who kept his nose buried in the grass. "I can't believe I've barely thought about her all morning since I got here."

She couldn't help feeling a little guilty for having such a good time with a new friend while an old friend was hurting. Still, it wasn't as if there was much she could do to help.

But maybe she should at least try. Maybe just being there would make Leah feel better. Remembering that she'd intended to go over to her friend's house to confront her after riding today, Nina decided to stick to that plan, even though she already knew what was wrong. Feeling better immediately, she gave a tug on the lead rope.

"Sorry for the short meal today, Breezy Boy," she said,

heading back to the barn with the reluctant pony in tow. "But I have a feeling Leah needs me more than you need more grass. I'll take you for a nice, long graze on the levee soon to make up for it—promise!"

Leah's family lived in a neighborhood known as the Marigny, which was on the opposite side of the French Quarter from Nina's house and the barn. None of the streetcar lines went that far, so Nina took the bus. When she climbed the steps to Leah's front porch, she was surprised to find the wide wooden floorboards covered in dust and leaves. When she knocked on the door, nothing happened—there was no sound from inside, not even the barking of Leah's yappy little dog.

Nina knocked again, and then stepped over to peer in the window. "Looking for the owners?" a voice called from the street.

Nina jumped, startled and a little sheepish at being caught peeking. "Hi," she greeted the elderly woman who'd spoken. "Sorry, yes. My friend lives here, and I'm looking for her."

"Ah yes." The woman nodded. "Little red-haired girl?"

"That's the one. Have you seen her around today?"

The woman shook her head. "She's not here. The whole family went to stay with relatives out in Chalmette for the week. Something about termites, I think, though I haven't seen any sign of the exterminators yet."

The woman tsk-tsked at that. Nina smiled politely and thanked her, though she was pretty sure that termites had nothing to do with why the family wasn't around. She hurried around the corner out of sight and then called Leah's cell phone, feeling worried anew. Why would Leah's family move out of their nice home to stay with relatives way out in Chalmette? Were they really so poor that they couldn't even afford to keep the lights on, or was her father trying to avoid the police?

After two or three rings, Leah answered with a curt "Nina? What's up?"

"Hi." Nina pressed the phone to her ear, leaning back against a wrought-iron gate around somebody's front porch. "I'm at your house, and a neighbor said you're staying with relatives."

"That's right. Mom freaked out and wanted to be near her sister. So what are you, a private investigator now?"

Leah sounded cranky, but Nina ignored that. "Anyway, I'm glad you answered," she began.

"Don't get used to it or anything," Leah interrupted. "This number won't work anymore when the contract runs out at the end of the month."

Nina winced, wishing she could do something to make her friend feel better. Then she realized there was one thing she could try. "Oh. Um, well anyway, I had an idea. Why don't you ride Breezy in Tuesday's lesson?"

"No thanks," Leah said shortly. "In case you missed the memo, I can't exactly afford to take lessons right now."

"It's already paid for," Nina said. "I get two lessons per week included in my board, remember?"

"Oh." Leah hesitated. "Well, that doesn't matter. I still don't want to come."

"Are you sure?" Nina switched her phone to the other ear. "Jordan just told me she can't ride on Tuesday, so it'll just be us. And we can come up with some kind of story to explain to Miss Adaline why you're riding Breezy. Come on, it'll be fun!"

This time Leah was quiet for so long that Nina started to worry that she'd hung up. But finally she spoke. "Really? You'd be okay letting me take your lesson? For free?"

"Of course!" Nina said. "I want you to. Riding always makes me feel better when I'm down, and I bet it'll help you too."

"I doubt it." But there was no rancor in Leah's words this time. "Um, but okay, maybe I'll do it. Thanks, Nina."

"You're welcome." Nina smiled into the phone. "By the way, that trip to the Expo is all expenses paid too, remember? And I still have a ticket with your name on it if you want it."

"I don't know." Leah's voice went guarded again. "I'll have to think about it."

"Okay." Nina wanted to push—she was sure it would do Leah good to get out and have fun for the day—but held back. "Just let me know when you can."

CHAPTER
10

"KEEP AFTER HIM, LEAH!" MISS ADALINE hollered across the ring on Tuesday afternoon. "He's lazier than Ringo, you have to push or he'll stall out on you."

"Yeah, I know," Leah said, giving Breezy a kick to keep him moving. "Get moving, Breezy!"

Nina leaned on the fence, watching her friend's lesson. Miss Adaline hadn't asked too many questions about why Nina was letting Leah ride Breezy in the lesson. And Nina's guess had been right—even though Breezy was making Leah work hard, she looked happier than Nina had seen her lately. No wonder she'd been sneaking out and riding him half the night!

But was offering rides on her pony really the only way Nina could help her friend? She wasn't sure. The rest of the Pony Post had been helping her try to think of other things she could do all weekend. So far, though, they'd come up short.

The only thing they could all agree on was that made sense for Nina to talk to her parents about it. As Maddie had pointed out, Nina's dad was an attorney. Maybe he'd know how to help Leah's dad.

There was just one problem with that plan. Leah had sworn Nina to secrecy. She couldn't tell anyone what was going on. It was bad enough that she'd told the Pony Post—if she breathed a word about all this to her parents, Leah would probably never speak to her again.

Still, the idea kept running through her head throughout the rest of the lesson. When they finished, she suggested taking Breezy out to graze on the levee.

"Sure." Leah sounded more relaxed than she had all week. "Come on, Breezy boy, let's go find you some yummy green stuff."

They chatted about the lesson as they walked along

the tree-lined trail leading out to the levee. The broad expanse of sun-warmed grass leading down to the banks of the Mississippi River wasn't very crowded, since it was still too early for the after-work joggers and other visitors to arrive. There were just a few parents or nannies with little kids, a guy walking his dog, and a few college and high school kids lounging on the grass. That made it easy to find a good spot for Breezy to graze.

Once he was settled and busy cropping at the bright green grass, Nina shot Leah a sidelong glance. "Listen," she said. "I've been thinking. . . ."

"That's never a good idea," Leah joked.

"No, seriously." Nina took a deep breath. "Look, you can totally say no if you want to, okay? But I was wondering—do you want me to tell my dad what's going on? You know, with your dad's business problems? He's a lawyer, and he deals with stuff like that all the—"

"You promised!" Leah broke in, her voice panicky. "You didn't tell him, did you? Tell me you didn't, Nina!"

"I didn't," Nina assured her quickly. "I swear. But I think it might be a good idea. If your dad's worried about going to jail, that means he should have a good lawyer, right? And my dad's a great one."

Leah glared at her. "Did I stutter? I said no."

"Okay." Nina couldn't resist one more try. "But if you just think about it, maybe later you—"

"Aargh!" Leah threw Breezy's lead rope at Nina so hard it smacked her on the arm and fell to the ground. Spinning on her heel, Leah stomped away without a backward glance.

Breezy lifted his head, staring back the way Leah had gone. Nina scooped the lead rope off the ground.

"Sorry about that, boy," she said with a pat for the pony. "I hope we didn't ruin your appetite with that fight." She smiled as Breezy lowered his head again, reaching for another mouthful of grass. "Okay, guess I didn't need to worry about that. . . ."

Her smile faded and she sighed, glancing off the way Leah had gone. But she was already long out of sight.

Nina was still fretting over Leah when she got home. The cats were asleep on a sunny windowsill, her mother was hard at work on a new sculpture in the studio, and her father wasn't home from work yet. Nina was glad that neither of her parents could see her just then—if they could, they'd be sure to notice how perplexed she was by this whole Leah situation. And she couldn't tell them what was bothering her without betraying her friend's trust.

But she needed to talk about it with *someone*. Luckily she knew exactly where to go.

Minutes later she was sitting cross-legged on her bed with her laptop open in front of her. She logged on to the Pony Post and was happy to notice that the last two messages—from Maddie and Haley—had posted only minutes earlier.

[NINA] Hey, anybody here?

She posted her message and sat back to wait. Before long she had responses from both her friends.

[MADDIE] N! How'd it go at the stable?

[HALEY] Hi, Nina! I'm still here too.

Nina could hardly believe her luck. It was rare for three members to be on the site at the same time without planning ahead.

[NINA] Sooo glad ur here! Lesson was good, after lesson not so good.

[HALEY] Uh-oh! What????

[MADDIE] Did you tell L what I said?

Nina opened another text box and typed fast, telling them about her suggestion and Leah's reaction. Again, it didn't take long for both her friends to respond.

[HALEY] Eeps! So much for that idea. . . .

[MADDIE] Wow, she rly doesn't want anyone to know, huh?

[NINA] Ya, pretty much.

[HALEY] What did she say exactly?

[NINA] Um, NO? Lol. Pretty much just that, only meaner. Sigh, hard to be her friend sometimes, u know?

[HALEY] U were being a good friend.

[MADDIE] For sure! And she is being totally unreasonable!

[NINA] What do u mean? She has the right to keep her secret, right? I mean, I only even found out about it sort of by accident.

[MADDIE] U mean when you caught her stealing rides on yr pony? & riding him so hard he was tired the next day?!? She should know ur a good friend since u didn't kick her to the curb then!!

[NINA] I guess

[MADDIE] Anyway, sneaking around w/ Breezy was wrong. And she's wrong about this too.

[HALEY] Do u think so? I was sort of thinking the same but wasn't sure if I should say it.

[NINA] What do you mean?

[HALEY] U should still talk to your dad. It's the only way to help.

[MADDIE] I think so too. Won't u feel bad if her dad ends up in jail?

[NINA] Sure. But I'll feel bad if Leah never talks to me again too.

[MADDIE] I know. But she will see that u are right eventually.

[HALEY] And that u were trying to be a good friend.

[NINA] What kind of friend am I if I won't even keep her secret, tho?

[MADDIE] The kind who will do whatever it takes to help her. Even if she doesn't appreciate it.

[HALEY] M is right. Ur parents will know what to do.

[MADDIE] I'm always right, lol! But srsly, Nina, it's what I would do.

[NINA] Even if she never speaks to me again?

[MADDIE] Even then. But she will.

[NINA] OK. Tx, u guys. I have to think about this some more. But I'll let u know what happens.

Nina signed off, her mind churning with what her Pony Post friends had just said. Were they right? Was it worth risking Leah's friendship to help her family?

"I just don't know," she murmured to Bastet, who had just nosed the door open and leaped onto the bed with Teniers right behind her. "I mean, maybe Leah's dad will figure things out on his own. . . ."

She sighed, wishing she knew what to do. But at least it helped to know that her fellow Pony Posters were there anytime she needed them to help her work through a difficult problem. Or any time their different time zones and schedules allowed, anyway. Nina stroked the cats' glossy fur, wishing that Maddie, Haley, and Brooke were right there in the room with her to talk things over some more.

Then again, while it'd be nice to have them there, she supposed it wasn't really necessary. They'd already told her what they thought. Now it was up to Nina to decide what to do.

That night at dinner, Nina didn't have much of an appetite. She picked at her food, still trying to reach a decision about the whole Leah situation.

For a while her parents were busy discussing a friend's upcoming dinner party. But finally her father glanced at her.

"Don't you like the pork, Boo?" he asked.

Nina looked up and forced a smile. "No, it's great," she said. "I'm just not very hungry today."

Her father raised an eyebrow and glanced at his wife. "Nina not hungry?" he joked. "Better call the doctor."

But Nina's mother leaned forward. "Are you all right? You've been awfully quiet this evening."

"Still fretting over who to invite to the Expo?" her father added.

"Yeah, that's it," Nina replied quickly. She'd spent several dinners during the past week discussing that topic with her parents. "I mean, the least you guys could've done was spring for a few more tickets so I could just invite everyone I know!"

Her father chuckled. "Sorry, next time we'll be sure to buy out the whole place."

"I thought you said you'd invited the new girl at school." Nina's mother reached for another helping of salad. "That makes three, right? Didn't you say you'd already asked Jordan and Leah?"

"Yeah. But I'm not sure if Leah's going or not."

"Oh?" Nina's mother said.

She didn't sound particularly interested. Both of Nina's parents knew that Leah could be moody; they wouldn't question it if Nina said something like "Yeah, she might have something else to do that day" or even just "She changed her mind about going."

But she didn't like to lie, especially to her family. Besides, maybe her Pony Post friends were right. Maybe she needed to be a true friend to Leah, to help her however she could, even if it was hard. Even if it meant the end of their friendship.

Nina set down her fork and took a deep breath, hoping she was about to do the right thing. "Yeah," she said. "See, she just found out something terrible, and I'm sort of wondering if you can help her, Dad. . . ."

Right after dinner, Nina shut herself in her room and grabbed her phone. Her finger was shaking as she punched the little phone symbol beside Leah's name in her contacts list. She wasn't looking forward to this call, but she knew she had to make it. She wanted Leah to hear it from her first.

"Nina? What?" Leah sounded distracted when she answered. "I'm in the middle of something."

"Okay, I'll be quick." Nina swallowed hard. "I talked to my dad tonight, and he thinks he can help your family. He's planning to call your dad from the office first thing tomorrow."

There was a long moment of silence. When it finally came, Leah's voice was ice cold. "You're kidding, right?"

"No." Nina clutched the phone. "I know you didn't want me to say anything, but I just had to try to—"

"I can't believe this!" Leah shouted. "I can't believe you totally betrayed me! You total jerk, you rat, you absolute loser . . ."

There was more after that. Nina held the phone out from her ear a little, since Leah's voice was pretty loud. But she listened to all of it without trying to interrupt.

Finally Leah seemed to run out of words. "I'm sorry,

Leah," Nina said. "I understand why you're angry, and I hope you'll forgive me sometime. In fact, I'll save your Expo ticket in case you decide you still want it. I really hope you'll decide to come."

The only response was a click as Leah hung up. Nina dropped the phone on the bed beside her. Then she just sat there for a moment, shaking from head to toe and hoping she'd just done the right thing.

◆ CHAPTER ◆
11

WHEN NINA LOGGED ON TO THE PONY Post on Saturday morning, she discovered that there had been no new posts since she'd checked in the night before. That wasn't so surprising in Maddie's case, since it was still pretty early out in California. But Haley and Brooke both usually got up early to take care of their ponies, so Nina had expected they might have visited the site already.

But she wasn't really focused on her faraway friends. The Big Easy Equine Expo was today, and Nina's local friends were due to arrive in about twenty minutes for the short drive up to Fair Grounds Race Course. That gave her just enough time to update the Pony Posters on the latest developments in the Leah situation.

[NINA] Hi, all! So I'm off to the horse Expo today—remember I mentioned that a few weeks back? I'll let u know how it goes. I invited Leah before all the crazy stuff happened and I'm rly hoping she shows up, but I'm not holding my breath. She hasn't talked to me since Tues. night when I confessed; she avoids me at school like I have Ebola or something, ugh. But I think it was worth it (?) b/c things are looking more hopeful for her family. My dad is doing all he can, and L's parents seem supergrateful (even if she's not. . . .). Last night Dad said he's pretty sure L's dad def. won't go to jail, at least, and he might even be able to get back some of their $ even if the cops never find his partner. So I'm glad I did it. I just wish L would forgive me, u know? But tx for the advice, u guys are the best! Gtg, will check in tonight. Hope u all have fun with yr ponies today!

After posting the message, Nina logged off and went to finish getting ready. When she got outside a few minutes later, she found her father standing at the curb beside an enormous white passenger van.

"Where did that thing come from?" Nina asked. "It looks like it's ready to transport an army."

Her father chuckled. "I borrowed it from your cousin Jeremy. He uses it at work to drive his crew around."

"Whoa, you mean you're planning to drive us uptown in that?" Nina stepped closer and peered inside at the rows of battered leather seats. "Seriously? Because like I told you, I'm pretty sure Leah isn't going to show, and Jordan and Edie and I aren't that big. Shouldn't we just take the car?"

"Nah." Her father shrugged, tossing the van's keys from one hand to the other. "I figure we'd better take this just in case you girls decide to buy another pony or a bunch of saddles or something."

Nina laughed, even though she still didn't really get it. "Okay," she said. "I'm just saying . . ." She forgot about the van when she spotted Jordan and Edie hurrying up the street. "Guys! You're here!"

Jordan broke into a run, flinging both arms around Nina and giggling. "I'm so excited I could burst!"

"Me too!" Edie danced from one foot to the other, then leaped forward and wrapped her arms around both of the other girls. "Thanks for inviting me, Nina!"

"You're welcome." Nina peeled herself out of the three-way hug and grinned at her friends. "I have some bad news, though. My dad decided to embarrass us by driving us up there in this school bus." She waved a hand toward the van.

"Cool!" Edie said, stepping closer for a better look. "We can buy as much horse stuff as we want!"

"That's what I said," Nina's father put in. "I'm Nina's dad, by the way."

While Edie introduced herself, Jordan giggled and elbowed Nina. "I just hope Leah doesn't refuse to be seen in something like that."

Nina gulped, realizing she'd never told Jordan about her fight with Leah. "Um, about Leah . . . ," she began.

"Here she comes now," Edie said, pointing.

Nina spun around. Edie was right! Leah was climbing

out of a car that had just pulled into one of the few empty parking spots on the block. Her father was getting out of the driver's seat.

"Hello, Stephen." Nina's father stepped out into the street to shake the other man's hand. "Come on inside. Girls, your chauffeur shall return shortly."

"Hurry up!" Jordan told him with a grin. "We have ponies to see, you know!"

Nina's father winked at her. "This will only take a second."

He and Leah's father hurried into the house. Meanwhile Nina stared at Leah in shock, hardly daring to believe she was really there.

"You came," she managed to blurt out at last.

"Yeah." Leah shrugged and shoved her hands into the pockets of her jeans, not quite meeting anyone's eye. "Um, can we talk?"

"Sure." Nina shot the other two girls a look. "Be right back, okay?"

Soon she and Leah were in the narrow alley between Nina's house and the one next door. A lush overhanging akebia vine blocked them from view of the street, and the neighbor's bubbling fountain provided cover for their voices.

"So . . . ," Nina began, for once not quite sure what to say.

"So." Leah took a deep breath. "I've been thinking."

"Never a good idea," Nina couldn't resist quipping.

Leah looked startled, then laughed. "Well, sometimes it's a good thing," she said. "Because I've been watching my parents, and they seem a lot, I don't know, more optimistic since they talked to your dad. So maybe it's good that you told him, even if I didn't want you to."

"That's what I thought," Nina said. "I mean, I struggled with the decision, you know? I really, really didn't want to break my promise. You've always been one of my best friends, Leah. You have to know that, right?"

"I guess." Leah reached for an akebia flower, stroking its soft petals. "And I guess you were just being a good friend by doing what you did."

Nina smiled, so relieved she could hardly stand it. "Yeah," she said. "I was trying."

Leah shrugged. "So did you give away my Expo ticket or what?"

Nina laughed, then grabbed her into a hug. Leah felt stiff at first, but then she relaxed and hugged Nina back.

"No way," Nina said. "That's one promise I did keep. I'm so glad you're coming!"

"Me too." Leah hugged her for another few seconds, then pulled back. "It'll be nice to get out of my aunt's house for a while. Thanks." She shot Nina a sidelong glance. "And, you know, sorry or whatever."

"No worries. Now let's go!" Nina took a step toward the street, then stopped. "Wait. How do you want to handle things? You know, with Jordan and Edie. I won't say a word if you don't want me to, but we should probably get our stories straight. . . ."

"No." Leah squared her shoulders, looking nervous. "You don't have to lie for me anymore. Come on."

She marched off before Nina could ask what she meant. By the time she caught up, Leah was already telling Jordan and Edie the whole story.

When she finished, Edie looked a little confused and

Jordan looked shocked. "No way," Jordan said. "That's horrible, Leah! I'm so sorry."

"Yeah, me too," Edie put in. "But listen, if you're worried about school tuition, I might be able to help."

"Huh?" Leah frowned slightly. "What are you talking about?"

"Edie's great-grandma founded our school," Nina explained.

"Really?" Jordan stared at Edie, looking impressed. "I didn't know that."

Edie laughed. "It's not usually the first thing I mention to people," she said. Then she turned back to Leah. "But seriously, my family still has some influence over scholarship awards and stuff like that. So even if things don't get worked out for your family by next semester, at least maybe you'll be able to stay at school."

Nina held her breath, afraid that Leah might get snippy about the new girl's offer. But Leah just nodded.

"Thanks, Edie," she said. "I'll let you know. By the way, sorry I haven't been more, you know, welcoming or whatever. I'm sure Nina has heard it all already, but I heard you've lived in some pretty cool places. Will you tell us about them on the drive up to the Expo?"

"Sure," Edie said, and Nina let out the breath she was holding. Okay, so it was obvious that Leah was ready to change the subject. But she'd done it in a pretty cool way. That just reminded Nina why she'd been so eager to help Leah. She really was a great person—just like all her friends, new and old.

Just then she noticed that her father and Leah's dad were emerging from the house. Both men looked cheerful, and they shook hands again before coming down the porch steps. Nina smiled, glad that she'd taken the risk of helping Leah—even if she hadn't thought she wanted the help.

"So let's hop in this great white whale and get going, then," she exclaimed, ready to put all that behind her and move on. "It's time to have some fun!"

Ten minutes later they were on their way. Nina had decided to tease her father by sitting with her friends in the very last row of seats, saying that if he wanted to drive a bus, he should feel like a bus driver. Because of that, it was hard to see where they were going.

Edie had just finished another tale of overseas life when Jordan leaned forward to peer out the window. "Hey, are you lost, Mr. P?" she exclaimed. "We're going the totally wrong direction!"

Nina leaned forward herself and saw that her friend was right. "Did you have to go around construction or something?" she guessed.

"Something like that," her father replied.

Leah pushed Nina aside to get a look. "Wait, isn't this the road to Metairie? You went the wrong way, Mr. Peralt!"

"Did I?" Nina's father glanced at the three girls in the rearview, looking amused.

"Yes!" Nina exclaimed. "Fair Grounds Race Course is back that way!" She jabbed a thumb toward the rear window, wondering if her father had suddenly gone nuts.

"Oh right." Her father nodded. "I guess I forgot to tell you girls we have another stop to make on the way."

"Another stop?" Jordan wrinkled her nose. "Where?"

"The airport."

"The airport?" Nina echoed, more confused than ever.

"That's right." Her father smiled at her in the rearview.

"We've got to pick up a few other guests who are coming to the Expo."

Nina traded a mystified look with her friends. "Other guests? Who?" she asked.

"Hmm. Well, there are three of them," her father said. "I believe their names are Maddie, Haley, and Brooke."

• CHAPTER •
12

NINA WAS SO STUNNED THAT SHE COULDN'T
respond for a moment. She blinked when Jordan poked
her in the arm.

"What's he talking about, Neens?" she asked. "Aren't
those your imaginary friends?"

"Y-yeah," Nina stammered. She undid her seat belt
and crawled up to the front passenger seat. Her father kept
his eyes on the road, grinning broadly.

"Buckle up, Boo," he said. "Safety first."

Nina clicked on the shoulder belt. "You're kidding,
right?" she said. "You just took a wrong turn and you're
kidding . . . right?"

"Nope." Her father shot her a look. "This is part of your birthday gift, kiddo. Your mother and I set it up weeks ago."

"You mean they're really . . ." Nina couldn't finish.

"What's going on?" Jordan called from the back.

Nina ignored her. "They're really coming?" she demanded.

"Uh-huh. Maddie and Haley are arriving soon on a flight from Chicago—Maddie transferred planes there so they could ride part of the way together," her father explained. "Brooke's plane from Baltimore was due in a few minutes before theirs—she's probably already waiting for us."

Nina's jaw dropped. "Oh my gosh!" she blurted out. "Dad, this is amazing! You're amazing! I so want to hug you to death right now—"

"But you probably shouldn't," her father advised. "I'll take a rain check for sometime when I'm not hurtling down the highway at sixty, okay?"

"Yeah." Nina grinned and blew him a kiss instead. Then she climbed back to rejoin her friends, practically bubbling over with excitement. It took her a few minutes to speak coherently enough to explain what was going on. But once the others understood, they were as amazed as she was by the big surprise.

"I can't believe your parents kept this a secret all this time," Leah said admiringly.

"I know, right?" Nina grinned, bouncing up and down in her seat. "And the others Pony Posters kept the secret, too!" Suddenly it dawned on her what that meant. "Oh! No wonder they didn't want to talk about the Expo!"

"Huh?" Edie said.

"Never mind." But Nina smiled as it all started to make sense. Her friends hadn't been envious when she'd told them about the Expo. They'd been afraid of spilling the secret that they were coming too! No wonder they'd all just avoided the topic altogether. . . .

The rest of the drive to the airport seemed to take forever. By the time they found a parking spot for the van and headed inside, Nina's heart was pounding so hard she was afraid it might burst out of her chest.

She scanned the crowds wandering around the arrivals

area, wondering if she'd recognize the Pony Posters from their photos. Was that girl over there with the ponytail Haley, or just someone who looked a little like her?

While she was peering at the ponytail girl, she felt a tap on her shoulder. "Nina?"

Spinning around, Nina saw Haley, Maddie, and Brooke smiling at her, their faces as familiar as if she saw them every day. "You're here!" she blurted out. "Oh wow, you guys are really here!"

Haley giggled. "We're here!"

The next few seconds passed in a thrilling, confusing, almost overwhelming chaos of hugs and exclamations and introductions. Leah, Jordan, and Edie took it all in stride, grabbing the visitors' bags to help carry them to the van.

"Ready to get moving, girls?" Nina's father broke in at last. "The Expo's already started, you know."

"Sure!" Nina smiled at him. "I can't believe you and Mom pulled this off! This is the best birthday gift ever."

"Definitely," Maddie declared.

"Yeah," Haley said, while Brooke just nodded, smiling from ear to ear.

Nina still couldn't quite believe they were really here. Maddie was just as vibrant and likable in person as she was online or on the phone, laughing and talking almost nonstop. Brooke was much quieter, but with a gentle confidence that matched what Nina knew of her from online. Haley was as bubbly and straightforward as Nina would have expected, with a quick, contagious laugh.

Soon they were all climbing into the van. Nina's three local friends took the back seat, leaving the other two rows for Nina and the visitors. Nina sat right behind her father, with Brooke beside her. Maddie and Haley took the middle row.

"Okay, driver." Maddie clapped her hands as Mr. Peralt climbed into the driver's seat. "To the Expo, if you please!"

That made everyone laugh, including Nina's father. "As you wish," he said, starting the engine.

As they pulled out of the parking area, there was a moment of slightly awkward silence. Then Haley cleared her throat.

"So," she said. "Were you surprised, Nina?"

"Was I ever!" Nina exclaimed, and just like that, the awkwardness was gone for good. The four of them started chattering again, updating one another on their lives and ponies.

"This is so amazing," Haley said, leaning forward to peer out as they exited from the highway onto the city streets. "New Orleans is definitely different from Wisconsin!"

"It's different from Maryland, too," Brooke said. "I can't believe we're really here! When Mrs. Peralt called, I was afraid my mom and stepdad would say I couldn't come."

"Tell me about it," Maddie said with feeling. "It didn't help that they called my parents the same day I got a B-minus on my social studies test."

Nina laughed. "But they said yes." She leaned forward and squeezed her father's arm. "I can't believe I never even suspected a thing. You and Mom are pretty sly!"

"Don't you forget it," her father joked. "But it wasn't easy to keep it a secret, I'll tell you."

Brooke nodded. "For us, either. Especially when you kept posting about the Expo!"

"Yeah." Nina didn't bother to tell them how upset she'd been when they'd ignored those posts. It didn't matter now—it had all been for a good cause.

They were still chattering nonstop when the van reached the racetrack where the Expo was being held. "Wow, it's amazing how much imaginary friends can talk," Jordan joked.

Brooke gasped. "Imaginary friends?" she echoed. "That's what my friend Adam calls the other Pony Posters."

"Us too," Jordan said, hooking a thumb in Leah's direction. Then she grinned. "No offense."

"None taken," Maddie said with a laugh. "And can you blame us for talking a lot? We've been friends for like two years, and this is the first time we've actually met in person!"

"Okay, that sounds like a good excuse," Leah said with a smirk. "But I'm thinking some of you might talk almost as much as Nina here does even without a special occasion to blame." She waggled her eyebrows in Maddie's general direction.

Nina laughed as Maddie pretended to be offended.

She couldn't maintain it for long, though, and finally confessed that Leah was exactly right.

They all climbed out of the van and headed inside. Nina noticed that Jordan, Leah, and Edie were walking together, leaving the four Pony Posters to continue catching up. She felt a flash of gratitude for her awesome local friends. She was also glad to notice that Leah and Edie really seemed to be hitting it off now that Leah was actually talking to people again. That was good. Leah would need all the friends she could get to help her through this difficult time.

Nina forgot about that as they entered the Expo and took a look around.

"Wow!" Haley exclaimed. "All this—all about horses!"

That just about summed it up. For the next few hours, they stayed busy rushing around from one amazing thing to another. They started out by wandering through aisles of merchandise for sale, all of it equine oriented. Edie bought a new riding helmet at one stand, Maddie splurged on a cute set of glitter pink polo wraps for Cloudy at another, and all the girls spent a few minutes trying on cowboy hats at yet another.

Then Brooke checked the program and suggested they watch a clinic on bombproofing your horse or pony. That was so interesting that they all pored over the schedule, deciding to see a gaited horse demonstration and then a jumping clinic. In between, they got distracted by a parade of huge, gorgeous Friesian horses with flowing manes and tails. When they followed the Friesians away from the main area, they discovered several rows of horses and ponies housed in collapsible stalls with signs on the doors giving their names, breeds, and other information. They were able to pat a friendly Arabian, a regal-looking Saddlebred, and several adorable ponies of various breeds.

"Too bad there are no Chincoteague ponies here," Haley commented as she stroked the nose of a stout chestnut American quarter horse.

The horse's owner, a mustached man in a cowboy hat, heard her and looked over. "Chincoteague ponies, eh?" he said in a thick southern drawl. "Now that would be something! Don't think there are many of those down here in Louisiana, though."

"Sure there are," Maddie said. "Nina has one—he lives right in the middle of New Orleans!"

The man looked surprised. Pushing back his hat, he scratched his head. "Is that right, now? Maybe you should bring your pony to the Expo next year!"

"Maybe I should." Nina smiled at the other Pony Posters. "And maybe my friends can all bring theirs, too!"

Hours later, the Expo was over, and the girls were exhausted. But not too exhausted to go to dinner. As one final surprise, Nina's parents had rented out the big back room at one of their favorite local restaurants. Leah, Jordan, and Edie came, and Trinity and several other friends showed up. Many of Nina's relatives were there, too—before she knew it, her cousin Kim was discussing dance with Brooke, who it turned out had taken some classes as a little girl. And Maddie was telling Aunt Iris and Uncle Michael all about life in the California wine country, where they were planning to visit for their next anniversary. DeeDee looked surprised to see Leah, but when Nina filled her in on what had happened, her cousin went over to introduce herself properly. Everywhere Nina looked she saw people she adored having fun and enjoying one another. What could be better than that?

"Coming through, y'all!" a waiter hollered, entering with enormous trays of oysters balanced in each hand.

When he'd deposited the trays on the table, Haley's eyes went wide. "Wow," she said. "Are those oysters or clams? Because I've never had either one before."

"Oh, are you in for a treat, darling!" Aunt Vi exclaimed, taking Haley by the hand and leading her forward. "Now, here's how you eat an oyster New Orleans style . . ."

Nina laughed along with everyone else when her friend's eyes went wide at the taste of her first oyster. Haley swallowed, then looked uncertain for a second, and then smiled.

"I like it!" she said, and the room erupted in applause.

"That's good," Nina said. "We'll see how you like spicy crawfish and jambalaya next. . . ."

Dinner lasted well into the night. Afterward, Nina and her friends piled into the van so her father could drop off the local girls at their houses.

"Don't worry, you don't have to drive me all the way out to Chalmette," Leah informed him. "I'm staying over at Edie's place. I called my parents, and they said it was okay."

"Really?" Nina blurted out.

Leah rolled her eyes. "Did I stutter?" she snapped, but she looked happy as Edie gave Nina's father directions to her house.

By the time they'd dropped off the last of the other girls, Nina was yawning.

So were Haley and Brooke, though Maddie seemed as bright and alert as ever.

"Aren't you the least bit tired?" Haley asked when Maddie paused for breath during a monologue about some cute thing Cloudy had done last week. "I can barely keep my eyes open!"

Maddie shrugged. "It's two hours earlier in California, remember?"

"Yeah." Brooke stifled a huge yawn. "We'll see how lively she is tomorrow morning!"

Nina's father chuckled as he cut the engine. "Here we are, ladies," he said. "Let's get your bags inside."

Soon they were all set up Nina's room. Nina insisted that she could sleep on the floor while two of her friends took the double bed. Maddie and Brooke had agreed to share the bed, but only if Nina and Haley swapped with them the next night.

"You mean you guys are staying another night?" Nina exclaimed.

"Of course!" Maddie rolled her eyes. "You didn't think we came all this way for one day, did you?"

Brooke giggled. "Yeah. We can't wait to see more of New Orleans."

"And meet Breezy!" Haley put in.

"Definitely!" Maddie and Brooke chorused. "We can't wait to meet Breezy!"

They got their wish the next day. Even after staying

up half the night talking, all four of them were up early, gobbling down plenty of Nina's father's homemade french toast and sausage, and then heading for the barn.

When they arrived, Nina led the way to her pony's stall. Breezy stuck his head out at her whistle, pricking his ears curiously at the visitors.

"Oh my gosh, he's so cute!" Haley exclaimed, hurrying forward to rub him on the nose.

"I bet you say that about all the Chincoteague ponies you meet," Maddie joked.

"So what?" Haley turned her head and stuck out her tongue at Maddie. "It's always true!"

Nina led Breezy out of the stall so her friends could get a better look at him. The pony nuzzled Brooke's wispy light-brown ponytail curiously, as if wondering if it might be edible. Brooke giggled and wrapped her arms around the pony's neck.

"You are so sweet!" she exclaimed.

Nina smiled as she watched all three of her best "imaginary" friends hugging and loving on her amazing pony—one of the four incredible Chincoteague ponies that had brought the Pony Post together. She was so happy she could hardly stand it. Did life get any better than this? She wasn't sure, and she wasn't going to worry about it just then. She was just going to enjoy the best surprise ever from the best parents ever with the best friends—and pony—ever.

◆ Glossary ◆

Andalusian horse: A very old breed originating in Spain, also known as the PRE—Pura Raza Española. The breed is similar to the Lusitano from Portugal. Both breeds are known as baroque breeds because of their distinctive conformation, with an arched neck and flowing mane and tail. Andalusians are used in dressage and various other English and Western disciplines, and appear frequently in movies.

Bombproofing: Training a horse to be brave and calm when faced with new or surprising situations. There are various methods to achieve this, many of which include desensitizing the horse by introducing it to a variety of obstacles in a structured environment.

Fly mask: A soft fabric mask worn on a horse's head that keeps flies and other insects out of the horse's eyes (and sometimes ears—fly masks can come with ear coverings or without). Passersby sometimes think horses wearing fly masks are blindfolded, but they're not—all fly masks are see through even if they don't look that way from a distance.

Forelock: The part of a horse or pony's mane that grows forward from between the ears and hangs down onto the animal's face.

Friesian horse: A breed that comes from the Netherlands. Like the Andalusian and Lusitano, the Friesian horse is considered a baroque breed, and has appeared in various movies. However, while Andalusians and Lusitanos can come in many colors, almost all Friesians are solid black.

Gaited horse: A group of breeds that are developed to be able to perform gaits other than the usual walk, trot, canter, and gallop. Called intermediate or ambling gaits, these tend to be very smooth to ride. Examples include the Tennessee Walking Horse, which performs a gait known as the running walk; the Paso Fino, which can perform up to three intermediate gaits; and the Icelandic horse, which is known as a five-gaited breed due to its two additional gaits, the tolt and the flying pace.

Haflinger: A breed of horse first developed in the mountains of Austria. They are sturdy horses sometimes used for draft work, and many are pony size. They are always chestnut with a lighter (flaxen) mane and tail.

Paddock boots: Ankle-height boots worn for riding. Sometimes also known as jodhpur boots.

Polo wraps: Stretchy bandages worn on a horse's legs. Polo wraps can protect the legs against minor scratches or other issues. They come in many colors and patterns. Polo wraps must be carefully applied to avoid injuring the horse's legs.

Rising trot (also called posting trot): When a rider rises and sits with each beat of a horse's trot. Rising to the trot is easier than trying to sit a bouncy or fast trot, both for the rider and the horse.

Vertical: A type of jump. A vertical is upright and narrow, usually consisting of poles or planks set between two standards.

Marguerite Henry's Ponies of Chincoteague is inspired by the award-winning books by Marguerite Henry, the beloved author of such classic horse stories as *King of the Wind*; *Misty of Chincoteague*; *Justin Morgan Had a Horse*; *Stormy, Misty's Foal*; *Misty's Twilight*; and *Album of Horses*, among many other titles.

Learn more about the world of Marguerite Henry at www.MistyofChincoteague.org.

Saddle up for a new world of classic horse tales!

For a full round-up of pony stories inspired by Marguerite Henry's *Misty of Chincoteague* visit **PoniesOfChincoteague.com**!

Simon & Schuster Children's Publishing · **A CBS COMPANY**